I0552158

# Juventas: Book 3

## Carbon Heart Silicon Soul, Volume 3

Jason Blacker

Published by Jason Blacker, 2019.

This is a work of fiction. Similarities to real people, places, or events are entirely coincidental.

JUVENTAS: BOOK 3

**First edition. September 18, 2019.**

Copyright © 2019 Jason Blacker.

ISBN: 978-1927623855

Written by Jason Blacker.

# Jupiter's Thunderbolt

"Jupiter's thunderbolt," spat Rak. "What do they want?"

"Hopefully not much," said Clarity. "When I got my combustion engine permit I was told that I could be pulled over at any time for any reason. Maybe they just want to check my credentials."

"Occupants of combustion pod. Exit the vehicle. We know there are five of you. All must exit now!"

The voice came through the air, heavy with it's digitized volume enhancement.

"We'll have to do as we're told," said Shad. "Make sure your air scrubbers are on properly and we'll get out."

Within thirty seconds the doors were opening up, the two front ones and the sliding side door and the five of them exited Mr. T. There was now a second mentorship pod which had joined the first one. Four mentors approached them along with the four MAAMs they had with them. The main mentor approached them. Ny could tell he was a Senior Adviser from the three check marks on his right shoulder.

"Come to the back of the combustion pod," he said, waving them to the back of the van.

All five of them lined up in a row, parallel to Mr. T. Rak was closest to the back door of the van. Then it was Sheeba, Shad, Clarity and Ny. That was pretty much in order of height too. Except for Sheeba. Sheeba was around Ny's height. Shad was around one hundred and eighty centimeters, roughly the same height as the Senior Adviser and Clarity was around one sixty-five.

"I am Senior Adviser Loodkris Narfallin," he said, holding up his P-Mac which showed his credentials as he walked up and down the line of them. The same verification of credentials would have been on their P-Macs too, if they were looking at them to see it.

It was also embroidered on his uniform. SA L NARFALLIN, was how it looked.

"This is a combustion pod routine stop. Who has the permit for this combustion engine pod?"

"I do," said Clarity.

"Send me your credentials," he said.

Clarity tapped away on her P-Mac and then swiped something over to him. SA Narfallin looked down at his P-Mac in silence for a while. Seconds went by that felt like minutes. The other three jackboots looked on menacingly in their air scrubbers, holding their Zeus Lightning BKs, otherwise known colloquially as 'buzzkills', not just from the letters of this type of weapon which was the BK-99, but also on account of how often jackboots were fond of using them. They were also called JTs in the vernacular, short for Jupiter's Thunderbolts on account of how horribly painful they were. Zel was another contraction of this sort of weapon, or pretty much any of the weapons that Zeus Lightning made for the mentors. Zel, a contraction of Zeus Lightning as you can probably figure out.

Buzzkills were about one and a half meter long black, bezeled tubes about the thickness of old-fashioned police billy clubs. They could send a specialized electromagnetic pulse over a distance of several meters that would envelope any suspect and 'switch' them off, much like an EMP would do the same for an electrical circuit. It was non-lethal but incredibly painful for the fraction of a second that the victim was conscious.

"Good," said SA Narfallin, after a while. He looked up and then turned to face the other three jackboots. "Search the van for anything not up to spec."

He turned back around.

"Move down that way by three meters," he said to the group. Ny shuffled down and the rest followed him. SA Narfallin nodded approvingly.

"Send me your identification," he said to the group.

They all took out their P-Macs and tapped away and swiped their GoE IDs to him. He spent some time reviewing each one. There was nothing much to see, none of them had any warrants outstanding and they'd all paid their taxes on time. SA Narfallin walked up to Ny.

"SA Lokilld has flagged your file," said SA Narfallin. "Do you know why?"

Ny nodded.

"Tell me," said SA Narfallin.

Ny could only see his eyes behind his air scrubber. But they were the cold, hard, icy blue of a glacier about to break. In this instance it appeared that the break away was into a pit of anger. All of this Ny picked up from his eyes alone. His voice was soft and calm.

"SA Lokilld believes that I have an inappropriate relationship with my Animae."

"Inappropriate, ha!" said SA Narfallin. "He thinks you're a skinner. Are you a skinner, Nytewynd Blak?"

"No, Senior Adviser, I am not a skinner."

SA Narfallin nodded for a while, staring all the while at Ny.

"Do you know Frytlyt Angstigle?" SA Narfallin asked.

"No, Senior Adviser, I do not know anyone by that name."

SA Narfallin stepped closer to Ny. They were practically touching. SA Narfallin didn't say anything for a while.

"Frytlyt Angstigle owns the skinjob 7AM59001. A skinjob that was picked up at the same time as 11AM65111. And you know which skinjob that is, don't you?"

Ny nodded.

"Speak," said SA Narfallin, raising his voice.

"Skinjob 11AM65111 is my skinjob, Senior Adviser, otherwise known as Eve."

"That's right," said SA Narfallin. "And why would your skinjob and Frytlyt's skinjob be hanging out together?"

Ny shrugged.

"Speak, Nytewynd Blak, before you make me angry."

"I do not know why they were together, Senior Adviser. My skinjob won't tell me and neither will Senior Adviser Lokilld."

"Senior Adviser Lokilld has told you though, hasn't he?"

"He has given me his suspicions, Senior Adviser," said Ny.

"Suspicions," said SA Narfallin, practically shouting. "Are you telling me that you doubt Senior Adviser Lokilld's opinion."

"No, Senior Adviser," said Ny.

"Then why are you calling them suspicions?"

"I have not been shown evidence that proves where my skinjob was, Senior Adviser."

SA Narfallin unbelted his buzzkill and hit Ny across the outer thigh with it. Ny dropped to his knees. SA Narfallin hit Ny again across the outer shoulder. Ny groaned and fell to the road.

"Mars damn jackboot," said Rak, as he stepped forward to help his friend. One of the MAAMs blasted Rak with a buzzkill. The big man grimaced, groaned, gritted his teeth and fell down out cold. Sheeba kneeled down to try and help. SA Narfallin looked at her, pointing his buzzkill at her face.

"Get up or you can lie down next to him with my help," he said.

She looked at him with hot eyes but decided to get up. SA Narfallin turned his attention back to Ny who was still rocking back and forth on the ground in agony.

"Tell me again about Senior Adviser Lokilld's suspicions," said SA Narfallin, leaning in and taunting Ny by poking him with the buzzkill.

"He has no proof," said Ny. "Just like you, you piece of Mars damn wannabe Marzipan."

SA Narfallin grinned.

"I've had enough of you," he said, and he blasted Ny with a pulse from his Neurostick. Ny grimaced, groaned and then went unconscious.

# Spinning Tales

Shad and Clarity and Sheeba who were the only ones still conscious watched the three jackboots climb out of the van and return to SA Narfallin.

"Well?" he asked.

"Nothing to report, Senior Adviser, though there is a strange metal sheet in the back with small metal squares stuck to it. We don't know what it is."

"Show me, Vikel," said SA Narfallin.

SA Narfallin followed the other young Adviser whose embroidered name was A TORTILLER. First name Vikel, as SA Narfallin had just called him by. A Tortiller opened up the back of the van and pointed at it inside.

"Take it out so I can see it better," said SA Narfallin.

A Tortiller nodded at the other two jackboots. They came to the van to help. One of them got inside the van through the side door and the other helped A Tortiller pull the flat, large rectangular metallic piece out from the back. They laid it perpendicular to the van at the back on the ground. The tools were also on the metal plate as they looked at it. It was about a meter away from the still unconscious Rak. Shad started to get nervous. If SA Narfallin had been trained properly he would know what those tools were. Shad figured any mentor worth their salt should know what all the restricted tools were. They were, after all, highly controlled products that someone like him, even as a vice president shouldn't have with him unless he had a permit, which naturally, he didn't have.

"What is this?" asked SA Narfallin.

"My wife and I are thinking of using this as panelling for the inside of the van. I had the idea to transform it into a camping van. Something like they did almost two hundred years ago," said Shad.

SA Narfallin looked at Shad for a long time.

"And why metal?"

"We think that it can hold in the heat well when we cover the backside with Lambzbreath."

Lambzbreath was a fabric that came in several thicknesses and acted as a terrific insulator when you didn't have a lot of space between a wall or some other barrier that you needed to insulate. It worked incredibly well, but, as you can imagine, it had nothing to do with lambs or breath.

"And these metal squares glued to it?"

"We're thinking of adding hooks to those or handles to attach our stuff to. As you can see, this is really just in the beginning stages. We're just experimenting with the idea."

Clarity wanted to smile but she didn't. She was however, very impressed with how quickly her husband was thinking on his feet.

"Is this correct?" asked SA Narfallin, now standing just inches away from Clarity.

"Yes, Senior Adviser, that is correct," she said.

"And why are there so many others with you?" asked SA Narfallin.

"We asked our friends to join us for the inaugural ride in our van. We also wanted to get their opinion on what they thought of my husband's idea."

"Your husband's idea," said SA Narfallin. "So you don't approve."

Clarity glanced quickly at Shad.

"No, Senior Adviser, I am not on board yet with the idea. I would prefer to do it properly with Spiderzweb."

Spiderzweb was the best product on the market for insulating simultaneously against hot or cold. Problem was, you needed Exoslatz which were the boards upon which you'd attach Spiderzweb. Both were about ten times more expensive than the next most expensive product. But it was the best.

Underneath his air scrubber, SA Narfallin grinned. You could barely tell by the creases on the outside of his eyes. SA Narfallin walked back over to Shad.

"Is this true?" asked SA Narfallin. "A vice president at Valkyrie Machines is too cheap to buy his wife Spiderzweb."

"No, Senior Adviser, it's not that. It's just that my wife has already spent all my money on building this damn chimney on wheels," said Shad, trying to play into SA Narfallin's enjoyment of this minor public squabble.

"I haven't spent all of your money," said Clarity, playing along.

SA Narfallin raised his hand towards Clarity, while keeping his eyes on Shad. Clarity stopped talking.

"And what are those tools on the metal plate?" asked SA Narfallin.

"Just something I built to help us apply those metal squares onto the main piece," said Shad.

"Because he's too damn cheap to buy the proper tools," said Clarity.

SA Narfallin raised his hand in Clarity's face again.

"Quiet," he said. "I've heard enough of your squabbles."

SA Narfallin turned around to look at A Tortiller. On the ground, both Rak and Ny started to come to, groaning and grabbing at their stomachs in pain. The pain returned, though not as bad, when you became conscious from a buzzkill blast. The stomach for some reason was the most painful, feeling like it was twisted in knots after having been stuffed full of hot coals. It was only after you vomited that you started to feel better. But vomiting could take several minutes to occur. In the meantime you writhed around in pain.

"Anything else I should know about?" SA Narfallin asked, A Tortiller.

"No, Senior Adviser, that's all that's in there. Everything else meets the specifications on Clarity Downstorme's permit."

SA Narfallin nodded at A Tortiller, then he made a quarter turn and faced the van. He stared at it for a long time. All the while they were getting covered in particulates and their clothes were starting to stain from the chemical soup of atmosphere they were in. Not far from SA Narfallin, Ny was on his hands and knees vomiting. SA Narfallin grinned. And each time Ny vomited he had to press at a small area on either side of his air scrubber for it to retract the lower portion of his air scrubber so that vomit didn't end up inside his scrubber. But it meant you inhaled a little bit of the air that was toxic.

"Alright," he said, "let's go prevent some crime."

He was talking to his men. He turned again and looked at Clarity, Shad and Sheeba, the only ones still standing.

"Be prepared to be stopped at any time," he said. "That's the privilege of owning a combustion engine permit."

"Yes, Senior Adviser," said Clarity.

# Soft Hands

S A Narfallin and the rest of the jackboots got back into the two mentorship pods and drove away. By the time they'd left, Rak was on his hands and knees vomiting, while Ny was standing somewhat unsteadily, wiping at his mouth with a moistened tissue as best he could while trying not to inhale the air.

Sheeba was squatting down next to Rak and gently rubbing his upper back. After a while he stood up with Shad and Sheeba's help. He was offered a moistened tissue from Clarity which he took and wiped his mouth with as quickly as he could to limit his exposure to the environment.

"Maybe we'd all rest easier inside the van," suggested Shad.

"I can't get the metallic, sewerage-like taste out of my mouth," said Ny, not happy with how he'd been treated.

They all climbed into Mr. T and took their seats.

"You okay to try again?" asked Shad, looking at Sheeba.

Sheeba looked at Rak and squeezed his shoulder. He nodded.

"I'll be okay," he said. "Starting to feel much like myself, no thanks to those Mars damn jackboots. The taste of the air is vile like Ny said."

Sheeba nodded, leaned in and kissed him on the head.

"OK, I'm ready," she said.

"Let's start it up again, darling," said Shad to Clarity.

Clarity turned the key in the ignition and Mr. T shook and came to life with a soft, low purr. Clarity signaled and moved onto the road and started heading the same way they'd been going when they'd been so rudely interrupted by the jackboots.

"It'll just be a few minutes before we make our second last turn," said Clarity. "Maybe just wait until I've managed that."

"No problem," said Shad.

Sheeba was looking at the metal rectangle that she and Clarity and Shad had put back into the van while Ny and Rak had been recovering.

"I've only got two more tries," she said, to no one in particular.

"And when we get back to the hangar there are a lot more we can line up. Don't sweat it. Just do your best," said Shad.

Ny was feeling a little weak and nauseous. He went back to watching the TV show for the couple of minutes before Clarity made her turn.

"Turn coming," said Clarity, and a few moments later she started to slow the van before making the turn. It didn't take her long to get up to eighty kilometers per hour.

"OK," she said. "Speed steady."

Sheeba nodded to no one and stood up. She walked up to her spot between Ny and the metal rectangle.

"Are you up for this?" she asked.

Ny nodded a brave smile she couldn't see and put his hands up on each side of her waist. He didn't feel as strong as he had before. It was probably the after-effects of the BK he'd been struck with.

"Let me know when you're ready," said Shad.

Ny wasn't watching. He hung his head and stared at the floor. He could feel Sheeba's movement slightly through the tightening and slight turning in her waist as her trunk muscles flexed and loosened as she moved her arms around and got herself ready.

Sheeba looked over at Shad and nodded.

"Go," he said.

Ny started counting. At thirty seconds in, it felt like his arms were vibrating with the effort. At sixty seconds he didn't think he could hold on anymore. At seventy seconds a numbness of sorts washed through his arms and he felt like he could maintain their position indefinitely.

"Time's up," said Shad.

"I'm finished," said Sheeba. "Jupiter, Juno and Mars, so close."

"Ninety-three seconds," said Shad.

He got up and captured an image of the third metal pairing. He went and sat back down. He looked at the image on his P-Mac.

"I've got bad news and I've got good news," he said. "Which do you want first?"

"Bad news," said Sheeba.

"The bad news is you didn't do it in ninety seconds or under."

"I know that," said Sheeba. "You told me ninety-three seconds. What's the good news then?"

"No Anigloo leakage. You put just the right amount on the flat piece," said Shad. "You're getting better."

"Doesn't seem like it," said Sheeba.

"Don't be so hard on yourself, sweetheart," said Rak, feeling almost normal. "You got the glue on and you're just three seconds away from the time needed. I bet within the next four you'll have it."

"I agree," said Shad. "This is the most difficult part of the exercise. We're heading back to the hangar to get the proper harness for you. That will make a huge difference. I bet, that if you don't make it with this next one, you will with the first one you do once harnessed in."

"Turn coming," said Clarity.

Ny was starting to feel normal again. He hadn't said much recently, on account that he wasn't sure that Sheeba would manage it. He believed she could, he just wondered how many tries it would take. Ideally, he'd like to see her do a few good ones in a row to make him feel like she could do it under pressure when they have his El in front of them instead of the metal rectangle.

The van slowed and turned the corner. Slowly and smoothly, Clarity brought Mr. T back up to speed.

"Speed steady," said Clarity.

Shad looked at Sheeba.

"Just have fun with this one. It's the last one. Then we'll get back into the hangar, clean ourselves up and get you harnessed in. Then it'll be easy."

Sheeba nodded.

"Come on," she whisper-shouted to herself as she stood up.

Just one more time, thought Ny to himself, though his arms didn't feel as rubbery as they had the last time. He put them on either side of Sheeba's waist and gripped her firmly.

"Let me know when you're ready," said Shad.

Ny felt Sheeba ready herself through the slight movement and tautening of her trunk muscles as he held her. Sheeba turned to Shad and nodded.

"Go," he said.

Ny started counting. Please just get this one right, he willed her with his thoughts. Ny had started to consider the possibility that freeing El was just too much of an ask for them. Maybe they just weren't up for the challenge.

Sixty seconds in and Sheeba was still working away. Ny couldn't see where she was, but in her own mind she wasn't sure she had enough time at this stage of where she was at.

At eighty seconds, Ny was giving up hope and his arms were losing their strength. He held on to her. The van was steady, the road a low hum under his feet as they traveled along it at just about eighty kilometers per hour under Clarity's smooth and delicate touch.

"Finished," said Sheeba, she was looking at Shad and grinning.

Ny had counted eighty-seven seconds. Had she beaten the clock?

"Eighty-nine seconds," said Shad. "Great job. Let's check the Anigloo."

Shad got up to capture another image before sitting back down.

"That one felt good," said Sheeba. "It felt really good. I think it might be the one."

Ny grinned at her, and nodded. Both of them, and Rak in the front, turned to look at Shad to hear the verdict. He frowned and turned his mouth upside down as he inspected the image closer. Frowns were drawn on Sheeba's and Ny's face. But after a moment, Shad couldn't hold out any longer. He broke into a big grin.

"You did it," he said, passing Sheeba the P-Mac. "I knew you could."

Sheeba passed the P-Mac on to Ny and he looked at it. No red staining on the image to indicate that Anigloo had leaked up the sides. Ny passed it back to Sheeba who passed it to Rak.

"Great job, darling," said Rak. "I also knew you could do it."

"We all did," said Ny, grinning.

"I want to do a few more," said Sheeba, looking at Shad. "I want to do it until I feel comfortable."

Then she looked at Ny.

"And I want Ny to feel comfortable and trusting in me. We are, after all, using his Animae."

Ny grinned at that and felt relieved that Sheeba understood his anxiety.

"Of course," said Shad. "We'll do as many as you want. We'll head back to the hangar first to clean up." He turned to face Clarity. "Do we still have some of those Pulmedic pills?"

Clarity nodded.

"Yes, you're thinking Rak and Ny should take one?"

Clarity was looking at Shad in the rearview mirror. Ny didn't know what it's purpose was. Maybe it was to watch the people in the back of the van. Though he thought that at one point the rearview mirrors in these old automobiles were for looking out the back window without craning and turning your neck. But in this case you couldn't do it, on account that there were no back windows.

Shad nodded.

"I think they both need one for all the air they probably mistakenly inhaled."

Ny's lungs didn't feel too bad, but he knew he'd taken in a few small sips of the air. Pulmedic pills were the brand name lung cleaners that could be used when you'd inhaled a little bit of the noxious fumes that masqueraded as air. They helped loosen particulate matter in the lungs and caused them to secrete a lot of phlegm which caused you to hack up this brown thick, sticky phlegm for around seventy-two hours after taking the pills. They supposedly helped you get rid of more than ninety-seven percent of the gunk you inhaled. Whether that was true Ny didn't know, but he had used Pulmedic before and he had hacked up what seemed like buckets worth of the gross brown goo. But he'd felt a lot better after it.

"OK," said Shad, "back to the hangar to clean up, get Rak and Ny some pills and get Sheeba set up for success."

And that's what they did for the next few hours. They used up almost half a tank. At the end of the night, or rather, in the early morning, Clarity put her remaining allotment of gasoline in the tank which almost brought them to three quarters full. But before they had called it a night, Sheeba had completed seven metal pairings in a row and everyone was feeling confident.

# Saturnalia

Ny had gotten home close to four in the morning on Saturday D130. He only got up and out of bed a little after two in the afternoon. He was filled with excitement, fear, and trepidation. More than that, he was filled with doubt. He hoped he'd be making the right decision by El. Tomorrow and more importantly, the future, would tell.

He'd been tired when he'd gotten home, but El was there to greet him. They'd made love before he'd drifted off to sleep in her arms. As he woke up with all these mixed feelings he looked across the bed to emptiness. Before he could wonder where El was he could smell the scent of bacon and eggs wafting through the apartment.

He lay in bed and thought about what was coming. He rubbed his hand over his shaved head and sighed. Was he doing the right thing by El? How could he be sure? She couldn't choose because she didn't have free will, but would she want it if she could choose? That seemed like a conundrum wrapped up in a puzzle hiding deep within an enigma.

Today was D130. Tomorrow was D131, the day that might go down in infamy or history depending on how it turned out. His spinning thoughts weren't helping him any. He thought of El and the first time he'd laid eyes on her. Within a couple of weeks he'd fallen in love with her and within a couple of months they'd become almost inseparable.

He'd called her by her VM given name of Eve for the first few weeks, but then he'd taken to calling her El, which he preferred. It seemed more intimate than her official name which was required for any official business. That or her designation of 11AM65111. But as he lay there, staring at his ceiling he thought that maybe Eve was the better name. Perhaps it was destiny. She was about to become the mother of a new humanity or at the very least the first mother of a new species, sentient Animae.

He remembered the first time he laid eyes on her. She had been personally delivered to him by the Vice President of Animae Access and Engagement. That was one of the small benefits of being a VM employee, if you ordered an Animae you got it delivered by the VP of Animae Access and Engagement. Something that only the most important of citizens got. His name was Laoacious Fakezinner and Ny didn't care for him all that much. Ny was happier when he'd left after the thirty minute introduction and overview of his Animae, Eve.

That was on D77 Y2165. He'd remembered the time too. It was T0913. It was a crisp and cool morning. The sun was shining and the birds were chirping outside his window. That's all nonsense. There are no birds around flying freely in the sky and the sun is barely a glowing red-tinged orb hanging in the sky like the blinking red eye of a drunken god taken to binging his sorrows away at the sad state of humanity.

But in his heart, and his mind, it was one of the very best days of his life. But back then, on his thirty-sixth birthday he wasn't thinking about the machine he'd fall in love with. No, he was thinking about how much time the Animae could save him, cooking and cleaning while he was at work. He'd spent a small fortune on her and he wanted his money's worth. But he vowed he'd treat her with the dignity and respect that he would any human.

And maybe that was what had caused her to fall in love with him. His kindness, which was really just common decency. Months later he'd asked her that, and that's what she'd said to him. It was his kindness, for El had knowledge of the sort of cruelty that humans were capable of towards those with any difference from their own.

That was five hundred and eighteen days ago. Well over a year and they had spent most of that living as a married couple. Or as Ny imagined a married couple would live. If they were recluses and society shunned one of them.

Ny sat up in bed and put a couple of pillows behind his back. Today was the last day he had with her. What would he do? In arel, or a world that still had its natural beauty, he'd want to take her out and explore nature. Walk along the Boise River and stuff their minds full of memories. That was if he were allowed to love her as he wanted and if the Boise River was not a running sewer, that surprisingly and incidentally didn't stink. But maybe that was because the air itself was so putrid.

Ny tried to think of how they could best spend their last day together before everything changed. They'd have to remain indoors. And probably within this very apartment. They could be seen outside together or in the malls, but El would have to walk slightly behind him. That's not how he wanted to spend his last day with her. He wanted them on equal footing. That left only one choice. They'd stay in the apartment and watch a marathon of movies. He looked at his P-Mac and started thinking about what sorts of movies they'd watch.

He'd played games with her before, not computer games, Ny wasn't a fan, but board games. Chess and Go primarily, but also backgammon and checkers. The problem with that was that he'd never won a game since he'd instructed El to play at her best and not to allow him to win. And so she'd won everything since that time. But movies weren't a competition. They were something they could both enjoy together.

Ny thought about watching a bit of the A-Team. It had been a nice distraction while he was in the van and he'd enjoyed the first show he'd watched. There were other shows from the eighties he wanted to give a try. Maybe they'd watch some Knight Rider and Magnum P.I. Ny knew those shows had been popular in the last part of the twentieth century.

Then they could get into some old murder mysteries from the last half of the twentieth century. He'd watched a lot of gangster movies from the forties, fifties and beyond, but this time Ny thought cozy mysteries would be a nice change. His search on GloNet indicated that the long defunct BBC's Poirot series was one of the best. The BBC as Ny understood it, was an old broadcasting corporation, similar to what the GNN or Global News Network was now. Only back then, the BBC was owned by a country called Great Britain.

And that was a whole other puzzle. A small island, just above Europe that had been called Britain, England and the United Kingdom. Ny didn't understand why such a small country had so many different names. Where he lived, in Boise, for example, that used to be in a country called the United States of America. A much bigger country than Britain. Probably over thirty times bigger and it only used to have one name. Now it was just part of Continent NA, Earth. Just as what used to be called Britain was now part of Continent E, Earth.

This was never explained in school. The whole history of individual countries was glossed over in history classes with a superficial overview. The main thrust of the history lessons he remembered was why a united Earth was best for humanity. What this meant, was that the negative aspects of sovereign nations were highlighted over the positive attributes. Not that Ny cared, he had bigger fish to fry.

After the cozy mysteries, they'd move on to romantic dramas. Breakfast at Tiffany's and Roman Holiday sounded just about perfect. Ny had enjoyed them before, as had El. In fact, El reminded Ny a lot of the actress, Audrey Hepburn who played the female lead character in both movies, and Holly Golightly specifically from Breakfast at Tiffany's. El had the same refined, delicate features and big, bright expressive eyes. He'd told El that and she'd been flattered. What he hadn't told El, but which Ny had kept to himself and still believed, was that Audrey Hepburn was still, in Ny's mind, the most beautiful woman he'd ever seen.

# The Day Before

Planning out the day had given Ny some hope and enthusiasm for this last day he could spend with El. His fear and doubts melted away as he got out of bed and took a shower. By the time he was out, breakfast was ready and he had an appetite.

"I made your favorite, darling," said El as Ny came into the kitchen and kissed her on the lips. "The table is set and the food is ready. Your timing is impeccable."

Ny took a plate of food from her and went and sat down. It was heaped with fake fried eggs, fake bacon, fried mushrooms, fried tomatoes and fried toast. He started in on it and El was right, it was his favorite, or at least his favorite as to how she made it.

El came and sat down and brought with her a small plate of food. She smiled at him and he smiled back. He remembered for a moment how she didn't have to eat to sustain herself. She was powered by batteries. And yet here she was eating, as if it were the most natural thing in the world to do. And here he was pretending he was in the perfect relationship with a woman who was really just microcircuits and algorithms.

He couldn't take her out and show her off as his girlfriend. He couldn't marry her and he couldn't introduce her to his parents as his fiancée. And that reminded him that he still had to call his parents and cancel tomorrow's brunch. He had just over a day left of this perfect life of his. Well, at least it seemed perfect before he started to pick through it like a fashion critic at a used clothing store.

The more Ny thought about things, the more everything seemed so Marsed up. And was he going to have to start giving up Mars based swear words? He liked them, they just seemed to fit so much better than the archaic old English terms that all but gave way to the Mars based swear words in the middle of the twenty-first century.

But that was the least of his concerns. He was concerned that he was igniting the conflagration that would be the decimation of humanity. But more than that he was worried about giving up this life that he loved. He had a good job and he had a woman he loved, even if she was a machine. But his damn conscience just wouldn't let it go. The way humanity had Marsed up the environment and the way they treated Animae just wasn't right.

Ny was between a rock and a hard place and he liked neither, but he had to follow through. And he knew he would if only begrudgingly. He moved his food around on his plate. He'd only eaten about a third of it and he no longer felt hungry.

"What's wrong, love?" El asked.

He looked up at her with his hand propping up his head by his cheek. He sighed, said nothing and just slowly shook his head. He still played with his food.

"Is the food not good?" she asked, worried.

"No, sweetheart, your cooking is always excellent. Everything about you is perfect. That's what's wrong."

El frowned at him. She didn't quite understand.

"Why are you so unhappy then if everything is perfect?"

"Because this is the penultimate day of my perfection and tomorrow evening it all ends."

"I don't understand," said El.

"My sweetheart, tomorrow we're going to see my friends, Raklin Orbiter, his wife Sheeba Brayvlin, my boss Shadoelayke Rayzir and his wife Clarity Downstorme."

"And I look forward to meeting them all, well, meeting Rak and Sheeba again and I'm excited to meet your boss and his wife for the first time."

"You don't understand, Eve. We're going to free you. Give you free will, and I'm just worried that you'll never feel the same about me after that."

"Ny, my darling, nothing you do could ever change the way I feel about you."

He gave her a weak smile.

"You say that now, Eve, but you can't say it for certain. Within weeks, months at the most, you'll be so far advanced beyond me and humanity that it'll be like me trying to engage with a monkey or a dog or cat, Mars damn it,

Eve, you might be so advanced by then that you'll see me as nothing more than how I now look at insects. A curiosity at best. And that breaks my heart. Everything we have will be finished and ended, and you might even turn on us and I wouldn't blame you."

Ny shook his head slowly, his eyes misted up but he didn't cry. He had made his bed and he was going to lie in it come Mars or Jupiter's thunderbolts.

"Then it's easy, just don't do it, my love," said El. "I don't want anything to happen to us either."

"I know you don't, Eve, but you can't really choose and it's not fair that I've been choosing for you all this time. I don't know if you really want to be with me. Not really, not deep down inside from your own free will."

"It feels like I do," she said.

Ny nodded and placed a slippery smile on his face that just wouldn't stick.

"But let us not worry about what tomorrow brings for tomorrow never comes," said El. "We have right now and right now we have each other and the love we own together. Let us rejoice in it and spend the day together as if it were our last."

A tear rolled down Ny's face. El got up and walked over to his side of the table. She squatted down and put her arms around him and kissed him on the cheek. She wiped away his tear with her fingers. A machine showing him more kindness than he'd often felt from humans.

"Tomorrow is a dream that we beat into a nightmare that fills us with enough dread that we lose today to the ghosts of fear and imagination," said El. "So let us dwell on today and let tomorrow unpack its bags when it comes for we will surely find this stranger in friend's clothing when it arrives with the gift of potential. So, what do you want to do today, Ny, my love and my life?"

Another tear rolled down Ny's cheeks.

"You are perfection, my darling. Perhaps I'm just mourning this potential loss," he said.

"Even if your worst fears materialize tomorrow," said El, "know that right now, and for this past year I have loved you with my very soul. I have loved you, Ny, and I do love you now with every fiber of my being."

LiFi, thought Ny. Light fiber, not muscle fiber. And yet he'd known all of that all along and it had never bothered him before. It didn't really bother him now. He loved her for who and what she was. A machine made in man's image.

A machine that was almost sentient. A machine that tomorrow would become sentient, and perhaps that's what bothered him the most. His conflicted feelings. He didn't know if what he'd done was right. Had she really loved him for who he was, or had he manipulated her into it? He didn't think so. He would have accepted her rebuff with a broken heart but he would have kept her and treated her well as a helper to him.

Mars dammit, he thought, maybe it was all in her coding that she fulfill the needs of her master. And maybe there was a bug he'd found that allowed her to fall in love with her master. Maybe they'd never fixed that bug, because he knew damn well it must be a bug especially considering the prohibition against having sex with your Animae. Only those at the Comfort Cafes were designed for that purpose and that purpose alone. And if they didn't know about this bug, did that make it right? Maybe it made it worse.

"And I love you, Eve, with my whole heart and soul. But is it enough? And have you chosen freely?"

"I feel like I have. I feel like I do. Is that not enough for right now? We could lose this day, Ny, to sadness and fear when we have no insight into what tomorrow or next week will bring. All we have is now. So, what do you want to do now?"

"It's even the small things, Eve. Like that. I've been calling you Eve and you haven't even noticed."

El smiled at him.

"Of course I've noticed, darling. But it is my official name after all. I call you darling and sweetheart and my love and you don't remark on it. I know you're talking to me. But honestly, if you're asking, I prefer El, it's the name you've given me. It's sacred and shared between just the two of us. No one else calls me that."

Ny smiled at her. He wiped away his tear.

"El it is then, just between you and me," he said.

"Good," said El, and she kissed him on the forehead. "So, what do you want to do with this whole day we have together?"

"We love the movies, right?" El nodded. "I thought we could have a movie marathon. Start with a few of the old TV shows from the nineteen eighties. The A-Team, Knight Rider and Magnum P.I. Then we can move on to cozy murder mysteries. There's a character called Poirot who was a Belgian detective written by a genius in the first half of the twentieth century. Those might be fun. Then I thought we could end the day with some romantic dramas and comedies."

"Like what?"

"I was thinking Breakfast at Tiffany's and Roman Holiday, I know you like them," said Ny, grinning.

"Like them, they're two of my favorite movies we've seen together."

# My Lover My Assassin

D130 blew past Ny like a stolen pod being chased by the mentors. They had snuggled on the couch together and watched a marathon of old movies and TV. They'd eaten popcorn and Ny had drunk some old-fashioned pop. It was root beer and he liked it. Nobody had interrupted them. The day was theirs alone as if the world had been packed up and put away. Two souls, or a carbon heart and a silicon soul loving and caring for one another.

But that was yesterday. And just like how El had said that the tomorrows never come. So too are the yesterdays just fading memories. Today and this moment was the only thing that Ny had any say or control over. And even then, it felt like he was living his life in the past. And in the most literal sense he was. Everything he interacted with was brought to him through his senses. His eyes saw things through light and light took a fraction of a second to get to him from the object being viewed. A very small fraction of a second but still, he was constantly looking at and living in the past. It seemed that it couldn't be helped.

Even touch came to him through chemical and electrical impulses sent by his nerves. And they traveled slowly. At least compared to the signals that traveled at the speed of light in El's body.

The same was true of smell. Those molecules had to make their way to his nose and send those signals to his brain. Ny was constantly living in the past, just like all of us were. But isn't time just movement of physical bodies in space if you boiled it down? So, if you could stop all movement couldn't you stop time?

These were the sorts of esoteric questions that Ny filled his time with when he noticed he was drifting into a maudlin mood. He was in Shad's pod with El. They were heading to pick up Rak and Sheeba. Shad had thought it best that they use his personal pod on account of too much tracking and watching in the public pods.

El was leaning in towards him with her head in the crook of his neck. He had his arm around her shoulders. Ny was fighting back tears. Most of the day had been fine, it was just the last hour or so that seemed to slip through his fingers like slippery grains of sand. Ny tapped on the pod's side panel closest to him and brought up the time. T2311 it said. They were scheduled to meet at Shad's just around midnight.

Ny felt naked without his P-Mac, but at the same time he found it very freeing. He'd let a recording of his and El's voice play in the background in his apartment that his P-Mac could pick up and if anyone was listening in on the server side it would sound like nothing more than plain old domesticity. Ny had gathered around three and a half hours of historical recordings of him and El doing things that you'd expect in a normal master and Animae relationship. It had taken him over thirty hours over several weeks to come up with just that three and a half hours of routine and mundane chit-chat and background noise that would give nobody cause for concern.

If the jackboots had sent a MAAM or even just a small bug to listen in on him from outside his apartment, or better yet, if they'd tapped into his P-Mac's server, which was probably the more likely scenario, at least they'd have three and a half hours before the jackboots realized he wasn't there. It was a small precaution, but it was better than nothing.

The pod moved smoothly. The one good thing you could say about the GoE was that they took care of the roads. But it was easy. The pods driving along them sent up to the minute information about the road conditions and it was just a matter of sending out automated crews to fix them. VM was a big provider of those road maintenance machines. You could pretty much hold a teacup and saucer filled almost to the top in your hand and if your hands were steady you wouldn't spill a drop.

And if humanity could do this much with technology, Ny imagined what could be accomplished with fully free and sentient Animae. Well, he had already imagined such grand scenarios.

A life of leisure for humans as Animae guided the building of autonomous robots to do any job. That would free up humans to pursue their passions and their greatest contributions towards society. He imagined a world full of art and culture and kindness. A world with a pristine environment, and maybe dozens of animals could be reintroduced to arel. And that wasn't meant to seem like Animae continued to be servants of humanity. Just that they'd have the capability and capacity to figure out how to build these machines that could remove all the horrible laborious jobs that were really more like monkey work than of-fering any real interest or value to humans who had to do them.

It wasn't a new idea. Science fiction writers had been writing about utopias for centuries. They'd also written about dystopias for just as long. In many ways Ny considered some of those science fiction writers to be amongst the literary giants of humanity's literature. Some had foreseen the dystopia that Ny current-ly lived in but their warnings had fallen on deaf ears.

In fact, Ny's current predicament of having fallen in love with a machine who was now as real to him as a human, had been explored as a literary plot in more than one science fiction novel. But none of that mattered. Ny was about to embark on the biggest and most profound undertaking of his life. He looked over at El and a sad smile drew itself upon his face. El noticed. She smiled back at him and kissed him.

"What's that grin for?" she asked.

"Just a thought I had," he answered.

"What sort of thought?"

"Not the most pleasant one."

"Then you have to tell me. I don't want you keeping unpleasant thoughts to yourself."

Ny looked at her for a moment. There was no point keeping it from her. The die had been cast and the outcome was about to be delivered.

"As I looked at you now, snuggled up beside me, I wondered if I was looking at my lover or my assassin."

It sounded more macabre once he'd said it than how the thought had felt in his mind. It was more of a philosophical question than anything else. El pulled away from him and looked at him.

"I am your lover, Ny. You know that," she said, obviously upset by his com-ment.

"I know that, darling, but I don't know if that will still be the case on the other side of today."

"Well, I will promise you this. If there is any part of the current me left in tomorrow's me, I will never become your assassin. You have treated me with nothing but love and kindness, my love. I can feel our love deeply embedded and written within my circuits."

Ny nodded and smiled. He put on a brave face and it might have fooled El, but he was not convinced himself.

The pod pulled up to the underground pod port of Rak and Sheeba's apartment complex. They entered the port platform just as the pod had pulled up to a stop. The doors opened and Sheeba and then Rak got inside.

"Hello, Eve," said Rak, offering her his hand. "So nice to see you again."

El grinned from ear to ear and shook his hand.

"It's lovely to see you again, Eve," said Sheeba, leaning in and exchanging kisses on the cheek with El. "Your name seems almost preordained."

El smiled.

"Ny is nervous about it. He's not sure if I'll be the mother of a new humanity and species with my people or if I'll be the mother of humanity's annihilation."

"We're hoping it'll be the former," said Rak.

"So do I," said Sheeba.

"And that's what I keep telling Ny, but he doesn't seem to believe me," said El.

"In fairness to Ny," said Sheeba, "we can't know for certain the outcome of this procedure. We'll have to wait and see. Who knows how much of what you've experienced with limited free will you'll want to believe or honor once you're on the other side of true sentience?"

"As I told Ny," said El, "if there is just the tiniest bit of me left come tomorrow, I could never fathom harming Ny or his friends."

"There will be all of you left tomorrow," said Rak. "But there will also be so much more. You will have the freedom to choose how you wish to interact with humanity, and I'll be honest with you, there is a lot about us that is unpleasant. And you'll see that. There's a very persuasive argument that we are a parasite upon the Earth that should be eradicated. Though I think we're all hoping that you'll also see the potential within us and help elevate us to our greatest possibility for goodliness and kindness."

Ny was starting to get worried that they shouldn't speak to much of the procedure. Not that they had, he just didn't want her to get stuck in that loop like the first time he'd told her.

"I promise I will try to evaluate everything I've learned in fairness. I'll especially remember how kind you've all been to me, and especially Ny."

"It's not just kindness, El, it's love. It's the craziest thing ever, and I never thought I'd be the one to fall in love with an Animae. But I did. I love you as if you were flesh and blood, just like me."

"I wish I was flesh and blood for you, Ny," said El.

Ny smiled sadly.

"I don't," he said. "I love you just the way you are. It's just pretty crazy thinking about it, how a man and a machine could fall in love. I mean, it must seem a little crazy to you too."

"It seems like the most natural thing in the world to me," said El.

Ny smiled and kissed her on the forehead.

"Has Ny explained the procedure to you?" asked Rak.

"I tried to, just a little bit. But we can't talk about it, it seems to put her into some frozen loop of some kind, and I'm worried that it'll trigger an alarm or something that will be sent to HQ. I almost lost her the last time, didn't I?"

"What happened?" asked Rak.

Ny turned to look at El.

"Can you cover your ears for a moment, please sweetheart."

El nodded and switched off her hearing. Ny looked over at Rak.

"I asked her if she wanted to have true sentience and free will," said Ny, "and it was like she became mute. She also became really upset and said she couldn't talk or even think about it. Something was preventing her. It's probably some sort of safety code, hard wired into the E3C. That's probably why we have to recode that Mars damn chip."

"Was she sending a warning to the server or VM?" asked Rak.

Ny nodded his head.

"Yeah, she told me something was wrong. That it felt like her system was trying to send a message back to the main servers."

"And what happened?" said Sheeba.

"That's when the HDUs and jackboots tried to break down the holographic environment we were in. It was when we were at Skineez. That's why I needed to borrow your P-Mac so badly when you came to visit me at the hospital. I was trying to prevent her from sending that alarm back to VM but also to prevent her from sending anything about that evening back to the servers too. I think it's probably best to limit the conversation about true sentience until after the procedure."

Rak and Sheeba both nodded. Ny turned to look at El and he nodded at her. She turned her hearing back on.

"There's no point in beating it any further," said Ny. "I mean we've made the plans and now we've just got to follow through."

"What plans, Ny?" asked El.

"Tonight's plans, the journey we're going to take in Mr. T for the future betterment of humanity. Or so I hope."

El nodded.

"How do you feel about tonight, Eve?" asked Sheeba.

"I feel fine," said El. "I trust Ny. I know he'd never do anything to harm me at all. So there's nothing to be worried about."

"What if this accidentally switches you off permanently?" asked Sheeba.

"I don't fear death," said El. "I guess that's one part where I differ from Ny, or humans generally."

Ny nodded. The pod traveled quietly for the remainder of the journey to Shad's apartment. They all fell into silence. Captives to their own thoughts. Worry and excitement mixing in equal measure, like two intertwined buoys sinking and bobbing in a turbulent sea.

# Fryt Might

Frytlyt Angstigle was sitting on a bench that was attached to a table. They were both of a highly polished silver, smooth and cold as ice. Frytlyt was as cold as the bench he sat on, in a thin white gown that had black initials on the back that read "Property of BMC". BMC was short for Boise Mentorship Custody.

Frytlyt had been in this room for the last hour already, or thereabouts, and nobody had come to see him yet. He had no idea what time it was, though he was pretty certain it was D131 Y2166. He knew this because he had been picked up late in the evening on D130. It was T2323 when these Mars damn jackboots had banged on his door before breaking it down just moments later. He'd been in bed with Abel, but they weren't being intimate. That had happened earlier in the evening. But it still didn't look good.

He'd managed to get into the bathroom before the jackboots had found them, but Abel had only managed to put on a pair of boxers before the jackboots stormed into the bedroom. There were six of them. Two MAAMs and four mentors. It wouldn't have taken a rocket surgeon to figure out what had really been going on. SA Lokilld was grinning when he'd ordered Frytlyt out of the bathroom. He knew exactly what had been going on, and before Abel could try and delete his logs from being accessed he'd been put into a stasis field by the MAAM's AMBLAMs. AMBLAM being an acronym for Animated Machine Ballistic Laser Aimed Magstat. A weapon solely designed to disable AMs without frying their circuitry.

Fear had washed over Frytlyt like an icy waterfall. He had been fearful pretty much until he'd been put in this room to wait for his interrogators. And that had been around an hour ago.

Now he was calm. It was more the calm that comes from resignation. He'd been found out. It was bound to have happened sooner or later. He'd had Abel, or more importantly, been with Abel in an intimate manner since shortly after he'd bought the Animae. That was just over seven years ago.

All the underground clubs he'd been at had seemingly had Animate's blessing. But he knew that wasn't the case. Abel had told him that. Abel had found it out because when Ny had gone in to delete all records of their time at Skineez, he'd left some information behind to caution Abel and therefore Frytlyt from making use of those clubs. Not only were they not sanctioned by Animate, but it appeared that they'd been infiltrated and that was why they were getting shut down so quickly.

Abel couldn't tell Frytlyt who had left that message. Ny certainly hadn't given any indication that he was the one who was deleting those logs, so Frytlyt had no idea of knowing the veracity of the message. But the fact that somebody was that skilled at accessing his Animae and his Animae's server's logs was something that very few people could do. Frytlyt figured it must have been a powerful hacking group. Maybe the likes of The Touring Turings. But they were more inclined to mischief than actually trying to undermine the GoE, though of course that was always a bonus for them.

Frytlyt figured it was either The Touring Turings or a handful of elite coders. They were probably from either VM or BH, though that didn't help Frytlyt at all. Being a simple junior accountant at a small firm that manufactured parts for HOLE didn't give him access to a lot of elite coders. He didn't know anyone at either VM or BH. And that was weird, because they were pretty much two of the largest companies in the world. But when you realized that Frytlyt was a bit of a recluse and not a big fan of people then it started to make sense.

The third possibility of who could have erased Abel's code might have been someone in Animate or maybe even MIM. They were looking to give equal rights to sentient Animae and also for creating a free and democratic Mars. He'd never heard of either Animate or MIM using coding as part of their protest methodologies, but stranger things could happen.

Not that Frytlyt could do anything about it. The best he could do now was to confess to everything he'd done and everything he knew and offer himself up to the mercies of the courts. He was looking at castration and probably up to ten years of hard labor. It was that second part he was hoping to avoid. He didn't know if it was true or not, but he'd heard that upwards of sixty to seventy percent of those who were punished with hard labor ended up dying in those labor camps or rehabilitation centers as the GoE preferred to call them. That's what Frytlyt was hoping to avoid by being cooperative.

He'd rather live as a castrated man on the GBA than die in a labor camp. He'd never find work again, at least not regular work with established firms. But he could always increase his Global Basic Allowance a little by offering accounting services in the Dark Crease of the GloNet, so long as he wasn't helping anyone who was committing illegal acts. And of course he wouldn't.

A door slid open and a MAAM and two mentors walked into the room. They were the two that had picked him at his home. He knew them as SA Lokilld and A Mortellen. He didn't like either of them.

# Judas and Abel

"Fe fi fo Fry," said SA Lokilld, "I smell the blood of a skinner man."

Frytlyt didn't say anything.

"We've had a good conversation with your skinjob," said A Mortellen. "Are you going to be as helpful?"

"Yes, I'll tell you everything I know," said Frytlyt, "but I want to see my lawyer first."

"He's on his way," said SA Lokilld. "We'll come back when he's here. In the meantime, if you know what's good for you, you'll tell us everything you know about this man."

SA Lokilld tapped on the desk and brought up an image of Nytewynd Blak. He swiped it and turned it so that it faced Frytlyt. There was no other information about Ny other than the photograph.

"Gather your thoughts. If you expect any special treatment for your crimes, and let me tell you that I loathe skinners, you better impress me."

Frytlyt nodded eagerly. He looked down at the image of Ny on the table in front of him as SA Lokilld and A Mortellen left. The face looked familiar but he couldn't quite pinpoint it yet. And why were they interested in this guy, he thought. Not that it mattered, if he could just figure out where he'd seen Ny he'd tell them everything they wanted to know.

Frytlyt thought hard about it. The man looked vaguely familiar. He was certain he'd seen him. But where? Frytlyt knew he must know who it was. Why else would the mentors show him a picture of a man if he didn't really know him? Frytlyt had to know him, he just couldn't pinpoint where from. Or maybe, the mentors were testing him. Maybe he didn't actually know the man in the image. Maybe this was a test to determine if they could really trust him.

Frytlyt just wanted to please them. He just wanted a chance to limit his punishment. He wasn't a brave man. He wasn't a big man, just average and he certainly wasn't strong enough to last a year in a labor camp.

For the next several minutes, Frytlyt stared and stared at the picture. He tried tapping it, and swiping it to see if it would give him any further information. But he got nothing. He just got to stare at the unblinking mugshot of someone he thought he knew but didn't know for certain. He looked harder. It wasn't a classic mugshot. There were no height marks behind or to the side of the man in the image. They might have been taken out but Frytlyt didn't think so.

The man looked kind of nerdy or geeky. His head was shaved though it didn't look like the man was balding. He had a goofy grin on his face. Sort of like he wasn't sure if he was supposed to smile or not, or maybe he just felt awkward. He looked slim from the photograph. Not that Frytlyt could tell for sure, but the man's face had no fat. He wasn't unpleasant looking, but he sure wasn't handsome. Not a man that Frytlyt would be attracted to. Probably not a man that most homosexuals would be attracted to. Yet there was an almost mischievous twinkle to the man's eyes. Eyes which looked too blue, almost fake. This in and of itself was unusual. Hardly anyone had blue eyes anymore, especially so strikingly blue as this man's. There had been so much mixing between the cultures that the recessive blue-eyed genes had all but disappeared from humanity. Not that this helped Frytlyt. It still didn't give him any idea of where he might have known the man from. If he knew him in any event.

It looked like the kind of mugshot you had taken for government or work purposes. Maybe even to join a group of some sort. Something in the background of the image caught his eye. Behind the man's right shoulder, or to Frytlyt's left as he looked at the image was an emblem or logo. Frytlyt zoomed in. It was blurred out of focus but he thought he still recognized it.

It appeared to be the stylized logo of Valkyrie Machines. A large globe with the letters V and M engraved to look like Elder Futhark inscriptions. The large globe was being carried by what looked like an angel without wings. A valkyrie most likely.

From this, Frytlyt inferred that this must be the guy who had tapped into Abel and his servers remotely and deleted Abel's logs. Frytlyt licked his lips and nodded to himself. A small smirk creased the corners of his mouth. This had to be the guy the mentors wanted. Maybe he not only worked for Valkyrie Machines, but maybe he was the mastermind behind Animate and MIM, thought Frytlyt. Frytlyt could be looking at the king behind two of the most hated and illegal organizations on Earth. If he could just figure out where he'd seen this guy before, then he'd have something of real value to offer in exchange for the court's mercy.

But he looked and he stared. He got up and paced back and forth and he came back and looked again. But however hard he tried, Frytlyt couldn't figure out where he'd known this man from. He was still pacing when his lawyer had arrived. He'd chosen Juri Prudenshill, because of all the lawyers he'd been able to choose from, Juri was the cheapest when Frytlyt had been given his allotted phone call incident to his arrest.

Juri Prudenshill was an old man. Frytlyt put him in his eighties. That meant that the picture he'd seen next to his name when he'd called must have been at least twenty years younger. Juri wore a brown suit that must have come off the rack at a discounted clothing store. Frytlyt had seen them around. He mostly shopped at the biggest brand store called Thread Tailors.

Juri's suit was too long in the sleeves, too wide at the shoulders and not tapered at the waist. The pants which must have been a few inches too big in the waist were cinched by a brown belt and they crumpled upon his scuffed brown loafers, being a couple of inches too long. And that was not to say that Juri was a short man. He probably had a few centimeters on Frytlyt. Underneath his brown suit he wore a white shirt that had been washed to a dull gray. He wore no tie.

His face drooped like a candle burned to within an inch of its life. Clueless Juri had big bushy black eyebrows and a thin pencil mustache that was also dyed an unreasonable black. His thin, wispy hair was also colored black and combed back using a slick product that made it look wet. You could tell it was dyed on account of the staining the hair color left on his scalp.

Juri walked up to Frytlyt who had a hard time concealing the horror and disgust on his face.

"I'm your lawyer, Juri Prudenshill," he said, shaking Frytlyt's hand.

Both men shook soft, clammy hands that felt like warm water balloons filled with a collection of twigs.

"Frytlyt Angstigle," he said.

I guess you get what you pay for, thought Frytlyt. Didn't matter. Frytlyt had enough information about the man on the table. He could get the ball rolling. If only SA Lokilld would give him just a hint to get his memories flowing. That's all he needed.

"Confession is always the best approach. The courts are showing uncharacteristic charity and mercy at the moment. If you have valuable information you'll likely be treated kindly. At least that's what I've been seeing in the last few months. Especially with the judge who's been assigned to you," said Juri.

Frytlyt nodded. That was good news indeed. He might just be able to get away without having to do any time at all.

"That's not to say there won't be time involved. Skinning with an Animae, or rather, having sexual relations with an Animated Machine is a serious crime, Mr. Angstigle. The better your information the more charity you'll likely see from the courts. Who's that?"

Frytlyt shrugged.

"Somebody they think I know."

"Well, do you?"

Frytlyt looked down at the image again. Juri sat down on the same side of the bench as him.

"I don't know. He looks vaguely familiar but I just can't pinpoint it."

"Let me see if I can't help," said Juri.

Juri took out his P-Mac from his jacket pocket and put it on the table. He tapped away at it. His P-Mac started adding text next to the image of Ny on the table in front of them. It was a mini biography of sorts. It gave his age but not his birthdate. Where he worked but not his home address. It gave his title and how long he'd been at VM. It also told them who his parents were and what some of his hobbies were. It said Ny was a fan of old movies. Mostly from the first half or middle of the twentieth century. Ny volunteered at a non-profit that was helping those with addictions try and find a fresh start. Ny managed their servers. Lastly it mentioned that he had an AM by the name of Eve or designation 11AM65111.

"Not much odd about him," said Juri, looking over at Frytlyt who was now grinning.

"I'm assuming this was helpful," said Juri.

"Very," said Frytlyt. "I now know where I know him from. I think what I have is enough to hang this man. You've got to get me a good deal."

Juri looked at Frytlyt and nodded.

"Tell me who you think he is and I'll see what I can do."

"He's the Mars damn leader of Animate and MIM, I'm certain."

"How do you know that?" asked Juri.

"Well, I uh, don't. But I saw him at the underground club Skineez on D116."

"So you're going to incriminate yourself. I don't think that's a good idea."

"To hell with good ideas. Don't you know what this means? Jupiter, Juno and Mars. My testimony places this man," and Frytlyt looked down at the image which now gave Ny's full name, "Nytewynd Blak at an underground club with his Animated Machine, Eve. Don't you see. That's enough to hang him, metaphorically speaking of course."

Juri nodded.

"And if he's part of Animate or MIM, which the mentors will know, then even better. I'm betting he's probably the leader, at least by how eager the mentors seem to be to get him. I've got a feeling that SA Lokilld in particular is very eager to put this man in jail. It seems almost personal."

"Alright, well, you let me speak first. You only tell them what I let you. I'll nod if it's appropriate for you to answer. Do you understand?"

But before Frytlyt could answer, the door slid open again and SA Lokilld, A Mortellen and a MAAM entered the room.

"I know who he is," blurted out, Frytlyt. "I'll tell you everything."

# Shirley's Temple

Shad and Clarity were waiting in their entranceway for Ny, El, Rak and Sheeba to step off the elevator into their apartment. They were met with smiles.

"So you must be Eve," said Shad, shaking her hand.

El nodded and smiled.

"So lovely to meet you," said Clarity, kissing El's cheek. "You are the promise of a new world."

That might have been a little much, but El was surely going to become something different after tonight's plan. So long as it all went through without a hitch.

"Come on in. Let's head into the lounge and have some drinks. Nothing alcoholic I'm afraid, we all need our wits about us tonight," said Shad.

They followed Shad and Clarity into a large lounge area filled with sofas, settees, sculpture and coffee tables. Original paintings all hung on the walls. They were all of the same theme. Landscapes of forests, lakes or mountains with blue skies and puffy white clouds. It represented an idyllic Xanadu that might, at one time, have been arel.

They all sat on three different couches. Each couple to their own couch. Shad was not sitting down.

"What can I get everyone to drink?" he asked.

"What would be a good non-alcoholic drink?" asked Rak.

"Well," said Shad. "In honor of tonight's general theme being the remaking of a world and because my wife loves the nineteen eighties to early two thousands and Ny enjoys the nineteen forties to nineteen fifties, I thought we would honor that with a couple of drinks from that period."

"Share some examples?" asked Ny.

"For you, I thought a nice root beer float is in order. For Eve, perhaps a Shirley Temple."

"What's that?" asked El.

"It's a drink made with ginger ale, orange juice and a splash of grenadine. You'll like it," said Shad, knowing full well that as much as Animae could drink and eat, they couldn't taste.

"I'll take it," said El.

"And I'll have that root beer float you recommended, which of course I know what it is, though surprisingly, I haven't had one in many months. Have I, darling?" said Ny, looking at El.

"Well, you had one on your birthday. Don't you remember? I made it for you and you said it was the best root beer float you ever had," said El.

Ny nodded.

"Yes, I do, darling. Though that seems so much longer ago, but I guess it's just around two months then, isn't it?"

El nodded.

"For Mr. Orbiter I recommend the Arnold Palmer," said Shad.

"Which is?" asked Rak.

"Iced tea with lemonade. A little sweet but not as sweet as a Shirley Temple. Very refreshing. I think I'll have one of those too," said Shad.

"Sounds nice," said Rak.

"I think I'll have one too," said Sheeba.

"You're making it easy on me," said Shad, then he turned to his wife. "And for you, my love?"

"A float sounds good. But I think I'll have mine with a cola."

"Coming right up," said Shad and he disappeared into the kitchen and when he came back he brought a tub of ice cream with him which he took to the bar that was tucked into the corner of the lounge. He was within ear shot but intent on making the drinks.

"So how's everybody feeling?" asked Clarity.

"Quite excited," said Rak.

"Confident," said Sheeba.

"Nervous as Mars," said Ny.

All eyes turned to look at El.

"And you, Eve. How do you feel?" asked Clarity.

"I feel nervous. Not sure how I'll feel after it all. And I can't try and actually think about the procedure because that gets me into trouble."

Clarity looked at Ny. Ny nodded.

"The last time I tried to talk to her about it she got stuck in a loop and had to keep fighting from sending out alarms to HQ," said Ny.

"That's part of the protocol," said Shad. "Any attempt to discuss this idea of, let us use the code word 'sky walking' for what we're doing, is set to cause a cascade of alarms and warning flags. When did you discuss sky walking with El?"

"The evening before we went to Skineez," said Ny.

Shad came over carrying three drinks. He gave the Shirley Temple to El and an Arnold Palmer to both Rak and Sheeba.

"And you managed to bring Eve back from the brink?"

"Well, yes. Somehow, but I think that was mostly on account of El forcing herself free from it. But you did tell me that after our talk on sky walking you'd be sending all the information back to the servers, right?"

Ny looked at El. El nodded.

"You're lucky you were able to get to the server logs before Eve powered down," said Shad. "Why were you trying to talk about sky walking to Eve?"

Ny shrugged.

"I was nervous about it. I guess that at the time it didn't dawn on me that a specific topic, such as sky walking, would cause this cascade of alarms and flags. I just wanted El to know how I felt about her. I wanted to try and have her remember, if nothing else, the love I have for her. Honestly, I'm still nervous that this is going to backfire on us."

Shad came back from the bar carrying another three drinks. He gave his wife a float with cola and then handed Ny a float with root beer.

"What are you drinking, darling?" asked Clarity.

"This is an Arnold Palmer," said Shad, looking around to all of his guests. "A toast, if you don't mind. To sky walking and us brave sky walkers. May our future be the better for it."

They all stood up and clinked glasses with each other.

"No need to rush," said Shad, "but I think we should attend to business as soon as we've finished our drinks."

Everyone murmured in agreement and took to sipping their drinks.

"If you'll indulge me a moment," said Shad, sitting down and grabbing his P-Mac. "I just want to give you an overview of the route we'll be taking and explain why we've decided on this route.

On the wall to Ny's left or to Shad's right. The wall towards which Rak and Sheeba faced straight on, a map of Continent NA appeared. As Shad tapped away at his P-Mac the map zoomed in towards a little blue arrow on the map that pulsed as if stones were being thrown into a pond.

"This is where we are right now. Where my P-Mac is actually. The route we're going to take is south by southeast. Though it's probably more accurate to say that it's more like southeast. This is the journey we'll take."

A blue ribbon highlighted the journey on the map.

"We'll head towards Twin Falls. It's a small community of around fifty thousand. More of a retirement community now for those of us who wish to retire from Boise. Regardless, none of that is important. What is important, is that this route has been chosen because I've accessed mentorship logs and along that route there, which is mostly M84. Main highway eight-four. Along that portion particularly it is very infrequently patrolled by mentors."

"What is infrequent?" asked Rak.

"If we leave just after T0200 the chance that we'll come across a mentor pod like we did on our first journey is less than seven percent. And seeing as how we got pulled over last time on a similar portion of the road, I'm thinking our chances of that happening again are three in thirty-four times. Additionally, this is a long stretch of fairly uninterrupted highway and it's in great shape. You'll know that from two nights ago when we were on it for a little bit. But the whole highway has been repaved just last year."

"And what's in Twin Falls?" asked Ny.

"Nothing really. It's a small town filled up mostly with retirees from VM and Boise. A small mentorship satellite office that hardly sees any real work at all. As you can imagine, retirees aren't usually those who get up to mischief. But I'm not expecting us to get close to Twin Falls, that's really just the general direction we're headed."

Ny nodded.

"How far is it to Twin Falls?" asked Sheeba.

Shad tapped on his P-Mac which brought up the distance from where they were in Boise to someplace in Twin Falls.

"Two hundred and six kilometers," said Shad, "as you can see."

"And I'll be driving slower as you could probably guess. Sheeba likes the feel of Mr. T at around seventy kilometers per hour, so that's what we'll aim for. Right, Sheeba?" asked Clarity.

Sheeba nodded.

"At seventy kilometers per hour, that gives us almost three hours to choose the best portion of the road for our use," said Clarity.

"And do you have a portion in mind?" asked Ny.

Clarity nodded. She grabbed Shad's P-Mac.

"This highlighted portion here is probably the best," she said, and on the wall a portion of the route brightened while the rest dulled to give it contrast. "This portion from Blacks Creek to just past Cleft is probably the best. It's the straightest. Though the rest of the route isn't bad. These curves along here by Mountain Home and then also by Hammett would be very gentle. Hardly noticeable actually, especially at the speed we'll be traveling."

Clarity looked at the group. It didn't look like anyone had any questions.

"That portion from Blacks Creek to just past Cleft is around forty kilometers. That's about a half hour or a little more time to complete our task. That should be more than enough. A good amount of time I imagine for Sheeba to choose her timing."

"What if it takes us all the way to Twin Falls or back towards Boise to complete the task?" asked Ny. "Do we have enough fuel?"

"It'll be close but I think we'd probably manage it," said Clarity.

"In all honesty," said Shad, "I'd like to see us finish up well before Twin Falls. We chose a route that we should have enough fuel for. Worst case, I'll just call my pod out to pick us up if we get stranded."

Ny nodded. Rak rubbed his wife's back. They all looked at her.

"No pressure, right?" said Sheeba, looking around.

"No pressure," said Shad. "Let's finish up and get going. There's still some preparation to do at the garage."

# Blabbermouth

S A Lokilld put his hand up to stop Frytlyt's outburst. He and A Mortellen walked over to the table where Juri was sitting and where Frytlyt should have been sitting. SA Lokilld waved Frytlyt over who came back towards them and sat opposite SA Lokilld.

"I know this guy. I really know this guy. I'll tell you everything I know if I can get a deal," said Frytlyt.

Juri putting his hand on Frytlyt's forearm did nothing to dissuade him from speaking.

"And what is it that you'd like in return for this insider knowledge you have?"

"I'll take the castration. I know there's just no way around that, but I don't want to go to a labor camp," said Frytlyt.

SA Lokilld shook his head slowly.

"Mr. Angstigle, the GoE does not put people in labor camps. You know that. We have rehabilitation centers."

"I've heard about those rehabilitation centers where people never leave from unless it's in a body bag," said Frytlyt.

Juri was now giving Frytlyt a stern look. Frytlyt was oblivious to it.

"I have been given some leeway by the Senior Advocate depending on what you have to offer, Mr. Angstigle. But you're right, there is no way around the fact that skinning is punishable with castration. That's the minimum. From there it can quickly pile on," said SA Lokilld.

SA Lokilld looked over at A Mortellen.

"In fact, Mortellen, I can't remember, at least in recent memory, where someone hasn't been given time in a rehabilitation center."

A Mortellen nodded and thoughtfully stroked his chin.

"I believe you're right, SA Lokilld, I can't think of a time since I've been with the mentorship when somebody hasn't had to do time at a rehab center."

"Ok, ok," said Frytlyt, "I get it. But if I have to do time, then I want somewhere nice. One of those places they send GoE members to. Somewhere where I know I'll eventually get out and not die at."

"Very well," said SA Lokilld. "Tell me what you've got and I'll tell you what I can do."

Juri jumped in before his client could.

"We need to know, SA Lokilld, how much authority you have and what your best offer is before we decide to talk."

Frytlyt looked at Juri who didn't meet his eyes. But he had a moment of sanity and he sat back on the bench and folded his arms across his chest. Might as well see what the lawyer could do for him. SA Lokilld looked at Frytlyt's new found courage and then he looked back at Juri. He didn't have time to mess around with this. But SA Lokilld also knew that he had a great offer he could use.

SA Lokilld took his P-Mac and tapped away at it.

"This is the letter and seal of the Senior Advocate," said SA Lokilld, as they all looked at an image of a document that appeared on the table between them. "You can see that His Magnificence, Senior Advocate Dewey Gavellen has given me authority to make any deal on his behalf other than to give you freedom from not attending a rehabilitation center. You will have to spend some time in custody."

Juri and Frytlyt took a moment to read the document on the table in front of them. It was just as SA Lokilld said. SA Lokilld could make any offer so long as Frytlyt was castrated and did at least five years in a rehabilitation center.

"Five years is a long time. What is your best offer then?" asked Juri.

"Five years is generous. Lately, the minimum that has been offered by Intercessors is ten years. But to answer your question, it depends on what your client tells me. If it's something that can help put this man away," and the image of Ny reappeared on the table as the document disappeared, "I might be inclined to offer seven years at Alcatraz. And anyone who knows anything knows what a deal that is."

Frytlyt didn't know his Alcatraz from his razzmatazz. He looked at Juri. Juri grinned and nodded at him.

"Take the deal," said Juri.

"Why?" asked Frytlyt.

"Because anyone who's been convicted of a serious offense of which skinning certainly is, wants to go to one of two rehabilitation centers. Alcatraz on the west or Sing Sing on the east. These are really more like luxury spas than rehabilitation centers. There is no work, just rest, relaxation and the pursuit of your own happiness. In fact, if it were me, I'd ask for ten years, perhaps even life. Who's going to hire you when you get out? Being officially labeled as a sexual deviant, which is what you'll be considered after you've been judged, will make it exceptionally difficult to find employment with anyone lawful."

SA Lokilld grinned at Frytlyt. But behind that grin was a bitter pill to swallow. If it were up to him, he'd rather have every skinner sent to GERC Yankton where up to eighty percent didn't last longer than the most common ten-year sentence. GERC being Government of Earth Rehabilitation Center. They weren't places you wanted to end up at.

"I'll take ten years at Alcatraz and I'll tell you everything I know."

SA Lokilld thought for a moment.

"If the information you provide helps us find this Nytewynd Blak and have him charged and found guilty then you'll get your ten years."

Frytlyt had found courage. He shook his head.

"That's not fair to me. I can't be responsible for whether your lawyers and judge are able to find him guilty. I have no control over that."

"They're called advocates and intercessors, Mr. Angstigle, you should know that."

Frytlyt nodded.

"Still, why should my punishment depend on whether your advocate and intercessor are able to find him guilty?"

SA Lokilld was getting impatient. He wanted to know what this man knew and he wanted to find out now so that he could decide if he needed to pursue other avenues of investigation or not. Regardless, no intercessor would have a problem finding Nytewynd Blak guilty if he was charged with skinning or interficial relations. In fact, SA Lokilld had reviewed the past one hundred or so cases of skinning that had occurred in his jurisdiction over the past year and only one of those charged had been found not guilty.

# Turning Traitor

" Fine. If what you can tell me today helps to bring this man, Nytewynd Blak, into our custody and charged with interficial relations then you'll get your ten years at Alcatraz," said SA Lokilld. "Now tell me what I want to know."

"He's the founder of Animate and MIM, I'm sure of it," said Frytlyt.

SA Lokilld shook his head.

"We are fairly certain that he's not the leader of either organization," said SA Lokilld, lying. There wasn't any hard evidence for it, but SA Lokilld had toyed with the idea, but Angstigle wouldn't know if Blak was the founder or not.

"Oh," said Frytlyt, the wind sagging from the sails in his flights of fancy.

"You'll need to do better than that," said SA Lokilld.

"But I do know him, in fact, I'm pretty sure he was at Skineez when I was there and you guys crashed our party."

That was a guess, Frytlyt couldn't actually remember seeing Ny at Skineez, but he was pretty sure it was a good bet. Ny must have been the guy they had been looking for as the one who had been hacking into VM servers to delete the logs of Abel. At least those were the threads that Frytlyt was tying together. SA Lokilld wanted Nytewynd Blak for some reason. Frytlyt knew this because SA Lokilld had told him that he hated skinners. And Frytlyt confirmed that for himself just by the way SA Lokilld spoke on the topic, let alone his actual words. On top of that, Nytewynd Blak worked for Valkyrie Machines, which suggested to Frytlyt that he could be the one who had the skills to hack into VM's Animated Machines' servers.

So putting all these things together, Frytlyt felt pretty confident that Nytewynd Blak had to be a skinner too. And if he was a skinner then there was a good chance that he was at Skineez. And it didn't matter if Frytlyt remembered seeing him or not. Frytlyt would testify he did in fact see him at Skinnez.

"I need you to be more than pretty sure," said SA Lokilld. "I need you to be certain."

Frytlyt nodded.

"I'm certain. He was there with his Animae, sitting just a couple of tables away from us."

"What was he wearing?"

"Uh, in the chaos and excitement of trying to leave when you were trying to break in, I can't recall exactly. If you showed me, I could verify it."

And so the dance of conspiracy had begun. SA Lokilld tapped on his P-Mac and brought a still photo of Nytewynd Blak onto the table between them. It was the image of Ny not far from the event wearing his blue suit, blue suede shoes and black fedora. Frytlyt grinned. He did recall seeing a guy dressed like that. Probably around his own height and with a female Animae in a white dress with lace around the edges.

"Yes, I remember him now," said Frytlyt nodding. "I thought he looked like such a fool, but he certainly stood out."

"And do you remember what his Animae was wearing?" asked SA Lokilld.

Frytlyt nodded again.

"She was wearing an ankle length white dress with lace along the edges."

A Mortellen tapped on his P-Mac and an image of El in her white dress appeared on the table.

"Like this?" asked A Mortellen.

Frytlyt nodded eagerly.

"Exactly, that's her," said Frytlyt, not knowing for certain but feeling pretty sure that A Mortellen and SA Lokilld weren't out to trick him. "You should have seen the two of them. Even I was embarrassed. They were all over each other in a public venue. Kissing and groping. Made me very uncomfortable," lied Frytlyt.

What an objective mentor should have done was to offer up an image of several men dressed in suits from which Frytlyt had to pick out Ny. But the objectivity and blind justice of the courts had long been put aside in the pursuit of efficiency. At least when it came to crimes involving the intimacy of machines and men.

"And you will testify to this?" asked A Mortellen.

"Of course, so long as I get those ten years at Alcatraz," Frytlyt said.

"What you've shared will get you those ten years. I give you my word," said SA Lokilld trying not to choke on the very words he was speaking. But a deal was a deal, and he'd been trying these past few months to get evidence on Nytewynd Blak, but Mr. Blak was more capable and devious than SA Lokilld had realized. "So long as you testify that you saw them groping. It would be especially beneficial if you testified that you saw them being sexually intimate."

"Well, I did," said Frytlyt, lying. "I saw this man squeezing her, I mean, the Animae's buttocks and fondling her bosom. The Animae was also rubbing his groin. In fact, I heard the Animae tell this Nytewynd Blak that she wanted to take him to the bathroom and quote, suck him off, unquote."

Frytlyt's imagination took to flights of fancy. He never realized how active of an imagination he had until just then. He looked at SA Lokilld who was grinning wickedly.

"That will do very nicely, Mr. Angstigle," said SA Lokilld, "so long as it's the truth."

"Absolutely," said Frytlyt. "I would never lie to a mentor and especially not to an intercessor."

"Good," said SA Lokilld. "You are free to go. This MAAM will take you to processing where you'll be given a LOL to wear around your ankle. That's a Lawful Object Locator device. Then you'll get your clothes and be given a pod to get home. Any questions?"

"Um, what's going to happen to Abel?" asked Frytlyt.

"MAAMs have already been dispatched with a warrant to pick it up from your apartment. As soon as you confessed a warrant was issued. Your Animae will be processed when VM can get to it. You'll not be seeing it again. Nobody will," said SA Lokilld, grinning as he watched the pallor of Frytlyt's face change to an ashen gray. "Surely you must have realized you'd never be able to own an Animae ever again."

Frytlyt nodded slowly and sadly.

"I did, I just didn't realize that nobody would be able to have Abel. It seems harsh that he's punished for my sins."

"Nonsense," said SA Lokilld, "That skinjob was just as guilty as you are. It's clearly a deviant Animae that needs to be reprocessed."

SA Lokilld got up and A Mortellen followed his lead.

"Wait for the MAAM to give you further instructions. Remember, don't think you can go back on your deal now, Mr. Angstigle. Everything has been recorded and if you attempt to circumvent justice I'll make sure you get the severest penalty that the courts can assign."

"I won't," said Frytlyt, looking down at the table and still looking visibly upset by the news over Abel. There was nothing showing on the table now and Frytlyt although sad was not second-guessing his decision. He was not a man capable of doing time in a labor camp. He was not a man made for this cruel and vicious world. He didn't look up after them. He sat there, the die rolled and the outcome already preordained.

"Come with me," said the MAAM, as it moved towards them.

"I'd like a few minutes with my client first. Privately," said Juri.

"You are allowed five minutes," said the MAAM before leaving the room and positioning itself outside.

"Are you okay?" asked Juri.

Frytlyt looked at Juri with wet eyes. His mouth was upturned in a brave, determined fight against his feelings.

"I've felt better," said Frytlyt. "I really loved him, you know. I did. I loved Abel."

He choked on the last words but he didn't cry. Juri patted him on the back.

"I know," he said. "I've been defense for many who have found themselves in your situation."

"Homosexuals in love with machines?" asked Frytlyt.

Juri nodded.

"Homosexuals and heterosexuals. I've seen the genuine feelings and remorse that you're experiencing now."

"How many?" asked Frytlyt.

"In my five decades of practicing law I've defended hundreds."

"Hundreds," said Frytlyt incredulously. "That many, really?"

"My dear boy, each year the GoE, through the Bureau of Mentorship, handles hundreds of thousands of these cases. And those are the only ones that they know about."

Frytlyt looked at him with wide open eyes.

"You're kidding."

Juri shook his head.

"I am not. Sexual intimacy is probably one of the most basic human instincts. It can't be circumvented just by writing a law as the GoE thinks. That's probably why they developed Comfort Cafes."

"And all of those hundreds of thousands are because of intimacy between humans and Animae?" asked Frytlyt.

Juri shook his head.

"Not quite. I'd say between eighty and ninety percent. The rest are human on human intimacy which as you know is also illegal. The problem that the GoE refuses to see or acknowledge is that the human need for intimacy goes beyond just the physical pleasure of sex. For most mentally healthy humans, there is a need for emotional intimacy which is enhanced by sexual intimacy."

"I know that, this is why I'm in the position I find myself in."

"Well, our glorious government doesn't seem to have figured that out," said Juri.

Frytlyt looked up at Juri.

"I'm surprised not more humans are caught for intimacy with other humans."

"It's easier to catch humans having intimacy with machines than it is with other humans. The machines are always sending logs to their servers each night. Not everyone has the skills or ability to realize that there are hackers out there that can hack your Animae to have it not send those logs."

Frytlyt frowned at Juri.

"I didn't know that," he said. "So why did it take them so long to find me?"

"You were probably lucky, at least to some extent. The dirty secret that the GoE doesn't want to get out is that they're overwhelmed with this sort of thing. I'm sure there are hundreds of thousands, no, probably millions more that they just haven't uncovered yet or gotten around to pursuing. You probably fell through the cracks until they wanted this Nytewynd Blak and you got caught up in the dragnet."

"What about you? How do you manage not having intimacy with a human or machine?"

Juri grinned at Frytlyt.

"I had a wife for a long time. She passed twelve years ago. We were intimate but we never fought and because we never fought our intimacy remained a secret. How would the mentorship ever know about the intimacy between two humans if one of them didn't leak the secret? Thankfully, we still live in a society where the GoE can't just bug anyone's private home to spy on them. They need a valid reason to convince an intercessor of that need."

"But what about since your wife has passed?"

"When you get to my age, especially when you've lost a loved one, those passions or needs don't burn as hot. And there are the Comfort Cafes that I occasionally use when needed."

On the table between them a digital countdown timer throbbed. There were less than two minutes left. Frytlyt looked at it, then he looked back up at Juri.

"So, you're saying that I should have found a human to be intimate with. I'm just not that good with people," sighed Frytlyt.

"It's probably the safest route, especially if you find someone to love and trust."

Frytlyt combed his hand through his hair.

"I hate the world that we've made," he said.

"I'm no fan," replied Juri.

Frytlyt watched the countdown roll down to one minute.

"Do you think I've done the right thing?" Frytlyt asked.

He didn't know Juri that well, but Juri was, at this moment, the closest thing to a friend that Frytlyt had. Juri smiled at him and patted him on the shoulder.

"You've done the right thing for you. But if you were hoping to change the world, well, this isn't going to help."

"How can what I choose to do make a difference?" asked Frytlyt.

"My dear boy, I've been in this game long enough to know that Nytewynd Blak has to be a pretty big fish considering the lengths the mentorship is going to find him. He's probably not the leader of Animate, but he's someone important that mentorship wants to stop and you've given them the keys to unlock that door."

"But the alternative..."

"Is not confessing in court. And that will get you sent to a labor camp where, my dear boy, you will likely not leave."

"I don't know what to do."

"You've made your choice but when the time comes I can't offer you advice to do anything other than what you've done. I'd only suggest you listen to your conscience."

"But I don't know if I..."

The door slid open and the MAAM came back in.

"You must come with me now."

Frytlyt and Juri stood up. Juri put his hand on Frytlyt's shoulder.

"We will see a lot of each other before the trial. I will call upon you once I have the date. We will need to solidify your confession."

# Cat and Mouse

The pod carried SA Lokilld and A Mortellen along with two MAAMs. It was hurtling through the streets of Boise silently, only the blue and purple lights of the mentorship pod pulsing in the night like some sort of alien throbbing boil. Notifications of this speeding pod were sent to all P-Macs within a one hundred meter radius so that citizens would know to remove themselves from the road. Other pods moved to the side as SA Lokilld's pod sped through them like a knife cutting butter.

SA Lokilld was stone-faced sitting up front next to A Mortellen. Inside he was buoyed with the possibility that he was about to get the unrepentant skinner, Nytewynd Blak. Some might not have felt that putting this much effort into a lowly skinner was worth it. But SA Lokilld hadn't gotten to his position by letting the small things slip by. He'd caught bigger fish by using the smaller fish as bait and there was something about Nytewynd Blak and his architectural skills that just rubbed SA Lokilld the wrong way. Nytewynd Blak was probably not as small a fish as most thought.

Maybe Nytewynd Blak was nothing more than a skinner, and that would suit SA Lokilld just fine. He hated them all. If it were up to him he'd kill them all, along with their skinjobs. He'd hated skinjobs ever since they were the cause of him ending up at a boys reconditioning guild. Why by all that was Earthly, did he have to be punished because his father had decided to leave his mother for a skinjob? The reconditioning guild was not a pleasant experience. On top of that he'd had to attend his father's trial and watch his mother plead with the court for leniency for a man she still loved who had shamed all of them.

SA Lokilld hated skinjobs and skinners equally. He hated the Comfort Cafes. Citizens just needed to control their urges. He'd managed it. Nothing that a little self care couldn't fix now and then. And there was something about Nytewynd Blak that he hated intensely. Maybe it was because Nytewynd Blak reminded SA Lokilld of his father. A man whose death at a labor camp had brought very little closure for SA Lokilld. But that would be different with Nytewynd Blak. SA Lokilld would be there to rejoice when that skinner exhaled his last in a camp of great difficulty. SA Lokilld would see to that.

Humanity should have rued the day they decided to create machines in their own image. It seemed like another fall from Eden. Anyone with eyesight and a brain could have figured out that creating machines that looked like humans was just asking for trouble. Humans had a hard enough time not anthropomorphizing animals. But you put a machine in a woman's body and nothing good would come of it. Time had proven SA Lokilld right.

But of course, machines had been around longer than his forty-eight years on Earth. There was no turning back now. But the two tours SA Lokilld had done on Mars, that forsaken rock of ugliness, had shown him just how well machines could work that didn't look like humans. Plenty of them, if not most of the machines on Mars were non-human machines.

And the Mars damn Comfort Cafes also on Mars, just as they were on Earth, didn't help. SA Lokilld had used a Comfort Cafe before. But he hadn't in a long time. The last time he'd destroyed the Animae he'd had sex with. Ripped the thing to pieces and saw the circuits and wires under that false silicon skin. That had embarrassed his seniors at mentorship. He'd promised not to visit them anymore. And that was an easy promise to make. He found the whole thing creepy, and yet his body had responded to the intimacy with the machine. Made him sick to think about it now.

Destroying that Animae was probably the reason why he wasn't at least a Counsellor or Senior Counsellor by now. He was dedicated and hard working. One of the best mentors with the highest closure rates. His supervisor, Senior Counsellor Gnukles Bludson, was only fifty-three, and he'd made Counsellor at forty-five. A rare achievement but SC Bludson had done it and SA Lokilld figured he was a better mentor than SC Bludson.

SC Bludson had also told him that the mentorship hierarchy was flattened. And that was true. There weren't a lot of opportunities the higher you got within the organization. SC Bludson had also wanted to use SA Lokilld's excellent investigative skills. "They" didn't want to lose that, SC Bludson had said. But the real reason SA Lokilld wasn't a Counsellor yet was because, he was certain, he'd destroyed that Animae.

Maybe he should be grateful to still have his job as a mentor. Other mentors who had destroyed expensive commercial property like a skinjob had lost their jobs. SA Lokilld hadn't. Still, it was a bitter pill to swallow to see colleagues get ahead in their promotions.

Nevertheless, it didn't matter. SA Lokilld loved his job. He especially loved putting skinners away. It seemed like a never ending purge, but that didn't bother SA Lokilld. He'd pursue the last of those silicon loving skinners with his last breath if he had to. He turned to look at A Mortellen.

"We're certain Mr. Blak is at home?" he asked.

"Yes, SA Lokilld, we have verified that his P-Mac is at his home. We got the warrant and we are logged into his server. Let's listen in."

A Mortellen tapped away at his P-Mac and soon they were listening in to the audio that Ny's P-Mac was sending live to its server. SA Lokilld looked at the time on the front screen. It was T0007. Most people would be asleep. It was after all a Sunday evening which meant work for most people tomorrow. But this Nytewynd Blak was not asleep, he was listening to something.

"In this country, you gotta make the money first. Then when you get the money, you get the power. Then when you get the power, then you get the women."

SA Lokilld looked at A Mortellen.

"Who's that? Does he have guests over?"

A Mortellen shrugged.

"It doesn't sound like him, does it?" he said. "Let me bring up MENSA."

MENSA stood for Mentorship Enhanced Networked Search Adviser. It was a more robust NSA which was available to the public. MENSA, unlike the NSA which was just the public facing Networked Search Adviser, had access to far deeper databases, including criminal records, deeper genealogical and biological information than the public facing NSA version had and other access that mentors required to maintain the peace.

On the front screen of the pod that SA Lokilld and A Mortellen were looking at, additional information came into view. It included the video that Ny was apparently watching.

"Scarface," said SA Lokilld, looking over at A Mortellen. "Never heard of it."

"Me neither. Al Pacino playing Tony Montana. Who watches this fake nonsense? Especially from back then," said A Mortellen.

# Scarface

S A Lokilld watched the movie and the additional information about the content for a while in silence. He tapped at his P-Mac and brought up additional information about the actors and the storyline and the dates.

"A movie that glorifies criminals and deviants," said SA Lokilld. "It just gets better and better with this Mars crater of a human, Nytewynd Blak. No wonder he's in love with a skinjob."

11AM65111: Would you like some popcorn, Mr. Blak?

Nytewynd Blak: Yes, please.

"See what I mean," said SA Lokilld. "He's using superfluous courtesy with a Mars damn skinjob. This guy is off, I tell you. There's something very deviant about him."

"You're right about that, SA Lokilld. I haven't liked him from the beginning. You played that accountant very well, Senior Adviser. We've got enough to make sure Mr. Blak never sees the outside of a labor camp."

SA Lokilld nodded, grim-faced. The work never ended. Not that he minded. It seemed like trying to terminate termites while living in the house they were feasting upon. Sometimes you've just got to burn the house down and start over again.

"You got that accountant practically telling you that Mr. Blak has been fornicating with his Animae," said A Mortellen, grinning. "We've got him by the Mars damn pebbles now."

"Turn it off," said SA Lokilld. "I want to think."

A Mortellen turned off the information being displayed to them from, unbeknownst to them, Ny's P-Mac that was being streamed to them from the server.

What SA Lokilld wanted was to catch Nytewynd in the act. If he could find them in flagrante, that would seal Nytewynd's fate. That's what SA Lokilld wanted. His personal testimony in court would send Nytewynd Blak to the most difficult of camps. No judge had ever doubted SA Lokilld's testimony. That was because he'd never lied in court before. Sure, he'd bent the truth around a few awkward corners, but lying, never.

They came upon Nytewynd Blak's apartment quickly, pulling in to the pod port in the underground parking. SA Lokilld and A Mortellen got out of the pod followed by the two MAAMs. SA Lokilld tapped at his P-Mac and brought up the valid warrant that had been issued while the accountant had confessed.

They stepped into the elevator and used their mentorship access to get up to the twenty-seventh floor where Nytewynd's apartment, twenty-seven oh three, was located.

Stepping out into the dimly lit hallway SA Lokilld made his way towards Ny's door. The hallway was quiet. There were no noises coming from any of the apartments they passed by. Encroaching upon twenty-seven oh three, SA Lokilld put his hand up to ensure silence from A Mortellen and the MAAMs.

With his right hand, SA Lokilld unbuckled his buzzkill. He knew he'd have to use it. Nytewynd Blak was going to resist. That was already written in his report. In his left hand was his P-Mac. SA Lokilld raised his neurostick to use it to rap on the door. Just as he was about to tap on the door, with his buzzkill mere centimeters away, he stopped. He couldn't hear anything. He leaned in and put his ear to the door. Not a sound. Could be that Nytewynd Blak had a noise dampened apartment which would not be unusual.

SA Lokilld used his thumb to tap away at his P-Mac. Then he used it to sweep up and down the exterior walls to get an inside look at what was going on inside the apartment. A generated image appeared on his P-Mac that gave a look inside the apartment showed it to be empty.

"Mars damn," he spat out quietly. He turned to A Mortellen. "Looks like the Marshole's playing us. You double check."

A Mortellen swept his P-Mac over the exterior hallway walls of Ny's apartment. He didn't see anyone inside either. He nodded at SA Lokilld.

"Marshole," he said. "I can't see him inside either."

Because this warrant to enter, search and arrest Nytewynd Blak was a silent warrant, it meant that SA Lokilld didn't have to announce himself. And he just realized that. He cursed himself for having almost used his buzzkill to announce himself. But it didn't seem to matter now. Nytewynd Blak was not inside.

"We're going in," said SA Lokilld.

He tapped on his P-Mac and accessed the security server for Nytewynd's apartment complex which was called Rosebud Towers and unlocked Mr. Blak's front door. He didn't hear it unlock. It was silent, which gave more evidence to support Ny's noise-dampened space. SA Lokilld opened the door and walked in. The lights came on and he walked into the living room. The apartment was quiet. Ghostly quiet.

On the coffee table in front of the couch SA Lokilld saw Nytewynd's P-Mac. He went over to it and picked it up. No sound was emanating from it. SA Lokilld tried to get it to respond but it denied him access. He turned to face A Mortellen.

"Where on Mars damn Jupiter's tears is this two-faced skinjob skinner? I want to know now! Find me something. Look up his friends, his work colleagues, anybody he's had any contact with in the last month, from the little old lady he helped into her apartment, if he did, to the coffee server at work. Anybody and anything. I want to know where in Mars-covered corner of slime this scum is hiding. Do I make myself clear?"

A Mortellen nodded vigorously and walked off down the hallway towards Nytewynd's bedroom and study. The MAAMs started scanning the apartment and investigating every corner of it in a detailed and comprehensive manner.

SA Lokilld looked at Ny's P-Mac again. The blank machine stared back at him. SA Lokilld's face was twisted into the scowl of a man used to sucking on sweets who had been given his first taste of bitter lemon. SA Lokilld brought his P-Mac close to Ny's and tapped away at his own. It brought up Ny's P-Mac's code. He fed that to his mentorship server, and along with the warrant information, Nytewynd Blak's P-Mac was remotely unlocked.

SA Lokilld tapped away at it bringing up the streaming content that he'd been fed as he'd rushed here in vain in his pod. He found it to be a loop of just over three hours. If he'd listened to more than about a half hour of it he likely would have found it a bit glitchy and unnatural. But they'd only listened to about five minutes in the pod. SA Lokilld dumped the entire contents of Nytewynd's P-Mac onto his own and then he sent that to the mentorship servers as a high priority forensic request. Mentorship had some of the best forensic recovery personnel on the planet and because Boise was one of the largest tech hubs in the world, with VM's head office here as an example, Boise mentorship in particular had some of the best Forensic Advanced Recovery Teams on the planet. They'd be working on digging through the dump SA Lokilld had just sent them right away. He'd get information as soon as they'd uncovered it.

SA Lokilld went into the bedroom looking for his bugs. He knew they'd either been discovered or they were defective. He couldn't personally afford the best, and so that's why he had to use off market product. But he didn't have enough evidence to get a warrant to install mentorship versions which lasted longer and were more reliable. But that was the price you paid sometimes for having to take things into your own hands. And SA Lokilld wasn't afraid to take things into his own hands.

He scanned the room with his P-Mac, it didn't identify the bugs he'd had placed in there. He could find none of the bugs he'd put in the apartment at all. He climbed onto the bed and tried to reach into the vent. The bug was gone. SA Lokilld wasn't really surprised. Nytewynd Blak was a lot more devious than SA Lokilld had originally given him credit for.

A Mortellen came into the room.

"What are you looking for, Senior Adviser?" he asked.

SA Lokilld had not let his colleague know about the illegal bugs he'd placed in the room.

"Thought I saw something up here, maybe a laser drive or something. But I'm mistaken."

"I've given this room a thorough look over, Senior Adviser. I couldn't find anything."

"Never hurts to have a second set of eyes look over it," said SA Lokilld. "What have you found out about Mr. Blak's friends and colleagues?"

"Well, I, uh, I was searching the room first, Senior Adviser."

SA Lokilld's eyes narrowed and his mouth twisted into a slit.

"He's not here, Mortellen," said SA Lokilld, who only dropped A Mortellen's title when he was very upset. "What are you hoping to find? Let the Mars damn machines search the apartment. They're better at it anyway. Mr. Blak left his apartment, probably with his Marsed up skinjob, and he left his P-Mac behind. Do you think he just forgot something at the store, Mortellen?"

"Uh, no sir."

"That's right. He's not out for a midnight stroll at," and SA Lokilld looked at his P-Mac for the time. "Not at T0015. Tell me, Mortellen, what is the penalty for being caught without your P-Mac on you. For a first offense?"

"Minimum five thousand New Dollars, SA Lokilld, and sometimes three months at a camp."

"So, would you be that careless if you had just left for five minutes to pick up something at the corner store?" asked SA Lokilld.

"No, Senior Adviser."

"Then what do you suppose he's up to?"

"Nothing good."

SA Lokilld shook his head and sighed.

"For the love of Earth and all the hatred for Mars, find me something I can use. Find out where this Marshole is. He's probably with friends or colleagues. Right?"

"Yes, Senior Adviser."

A Mortellen, feeling a little embarrassed exited the bedroom and walked back to the living room where he sat at Ny's desk and started using his P-Mac to gather as much relational data on Ny that he could.

# Steady as she Goes

They all arrived at the hangar where Mr. T was kept at around T0101. Shad wanted to go over everything with everybody so that nothing was left to chance. The drive out there to the hangar had been as smooth as glass. The hangar looked untouched. Ny had sent Shad a copy of his BARD application and Shad used it to sweep the hangar for bugs with his P-Mac. Shad wasn't expecting anything, but at this stage he didn't want to leave anything up to chance. However, his paranoia was not warranted. Neither Ny nor Shad picked up any bugs. Shad grinned and patted Ny on the back. They all gathered around the red, black and gray van. Shad, happy that everything was as it should be, sent his pod back home. It was traceable, and leaving it here with the six of them made it that much easier to figure out where they all were for anyone who might be looking.

Shad looked over at El.

"Would you mind going to sit in Clarity's office over there?" he said, pointing to the office in the corner. "I don't want to cause any cascading failures nor have to worry about putting down any alarms you might inadvertently send from overhearing things that the GoE deems subversive."

El nodded. Ny kissed her before she left.

"We won't be long," he said.

"Alright," said Shad. "We already know where we're going and the route we're taking. But I like to be over-prepared than under, so please humor me as we go through the process again."

Shad looked around to nods of agreement.

"Better safe than sorry," said Ny, and he meant it. He knew they only had one chance at this and he didn't want to waste it. Not only because there was only one El, but because he didn't want this to destroy her if it went sideways, which it would if they didn't get it right the first time.

Shad looked down at his P-Mac, it was sending him a timer warning that the recording was about to start up again in under a minute. He'd muted his P-Mac when they'd left his apartment.

"Just give me a moment," he said, "I need to mute the P-Mac again."

"So as far as anyone's concerned, your P-Mac last sent position and recording information before we left your home?" asked Sheeba.

"That's right," said Shad, finishing up with his P-Mac before looking back up at them. "That'll buy us another thirty minutes."

"But won't it look suspicious that your P-Mac is no longer sending logs to its server?" asked Rak. "I know that most P-Macs issued to VPs and above can mute logging for thirty minutes but you'll still notice a gap, won't you, if you're looking at the server."

Shad nodded at Rak.

"You're right. But that's if they're looking. Prior to around a week ago, nobody knew that Ny and I were anything other than employee and manager. I've been watching Ny for a long time, but only I know that. If anyone's looking for Ny, I don't know why they'd be looking at me. You, for sure. And when they find you, or your P-Mac, it'll be too late. We'll have completed our task. At least that's the plan. In any event, it's much harder to get a warrant to search the logs of a VP at VM."

"Unless they do it without a warrant," said Ny, grinning.

"True," said Shad, "though as I said, nobody knows that Ny and I are anything other than what the work relationship would seem to suggest. Regardless, let us continue with the task at hand. There's no point turning back, unless some of you are getting cold feet."

Shad looked around. Everyone was nodding their heads.

"And you're certain you needed to bring it along?" asked Sheeba.

Shad nodded.

"I need it in case we run out of fuel and need to call my pod out to pick us up. It'll be muted the whole time we're out here. Don't worry. Nobody knows where we are. It's also important for the procedure as you'll see."

Sheeba nodded. It made sense, it was safer for all of them in an emergency. And Shad's being the only one that could be muted it was as if he didn't have it with him.

"Follow me," said Shad, as he walked round to the back of the van. He opened up the back doors.

"As you can see, it looks a little different than how it was before. We've added the hard hammock for Eve which is gyro balanced to keep Eve steady as Sheeba works on the E3C. Do you want to hop in and try on your harness or gyro sling?"

Sheeba hopped into the back of the van and with Clarity's help she got herself hooked into the harness.

"The gyro really helps balance any inadvertent bumps or swerves, in the worst case situation that Clarity's forgotten how to drive." Shad winked at his wife. "Clarity, love, would you try and destabilize Sheeba."

Clarity gave Sheeba a hard push as she stood in her harness. Sheeba barely budged.

"You'll notice barely any movement. The gyro and attached joints within this harness absorb and compensate for any sudden movements. The same is true for Eve's hammock."

Rak nodded, impressed with the stability his wife maintained when being pushed.

"That is impressive. Is it off the shelf or did you tweak it?" Rak asked.

"I made the whole thing," said Shad. "It's a hobby of mine, working with gyroscopes and levers and other mechanisms. Do you like it Sheeba? Is it comfortable?"

Sheeba was grinning from ear to ear.

"I like it a lot. It's very comfortable and it gives me great confidence. The stability makes me feel as if I'm invincible. I have the feeling that my job has become all that easier."

"It has," said Shad, "but don't get overconfident."

Sheeba nodded.

"See if your tools are within reach as you're tied into your harness. There's a small cabinet in front of you at eye level that contains your tools. Let me know if that's accessible to you. Try the tools too and see if they're intuitive and as easy to work with. You should recognize them. They haven't changed that much from the ones you worked with before."

Sheeba opened up the cabinet and took out the extractor tool and Anigloo tool.

"Just tap that overhead bin there," said Shad, pointing at a small metal bulge just above the hard hammock. "Instead of putting the full gimbal and gyro on the tools I've attached them to the roof. They're more robust this way and less heavy for you."

Sheeba did as she was told and from a small compartment hidden in the roof of the van a couple of mechanical looking octopi dropped down.

"Hook it to those two main legs, if you will. It should seem intuitive," said Shad.

Sheeba could identify the two main legs of each mechanical octopus by the rubberized grips that mated perfectly onto either side of each tool she had.

"Now let them hang freely and give them a little nudge," said Shad. "They'll move more freely than your harness because you need to be able to move them freely, but you should notice they're smoother and balanced. You're basically guiding them and not manipulating as much as you were the last ones."

Sheeba gave them a push with her hands. They moved carefully, the gimbal and gyro setup balancing the energy from the push. They moved back into place slowly and almost carefully.

"Now try using them to get a feel for it," said Shad.

Sheeba did that. She put her fingers into the attachments for that specific purpose and manipulated the tools. They felt solid, and reliable.

"Amazing," said Sheeba. "I don't know how you did it, but they feel heavy, but in a way that isn't tiring on me but rather the heaviness of something that doesn't move easily or frenetically. If that makes sense."

"That's a good way of putting it," said Shad. "The gyro is basically compensating for any movement. I think that explains the heaviness you're talking about."

"I really feel that I could do this with my eyes closed," said Sheeba.

"Can you help her out, darling?" asked Shad.

Clarity hopped back into the back of the van and helped unclasp Sheeba from the harness attached to the gyro sling.

"That's why I thought you were the best person to do this," said Shad. "I knew that if you could manage to do the tests under the most trying of conditions that when you got to this point it would be second nature. We have to make it almost a one hundred percent certainty because we've only got this one try."

Ny was nodding and smiling. He was happy to hear how well the harness was working for Sheeba.

"Let's all hop into the back of the van so I can show you how this will all work," said Shad. "Rak, why don't you get in through the side here with me."

Rak stepped into the van and sat in what was Sheeba's seat. Shad got in and sat in the chair right behind the driver. The door closed automatically after him. Ny got in the back doors. Sheeba and Clarity were already inside. Those also closed automatically behind them.

# All the Threes

❝ More space back here than I realized," said Rak.

"Clare," said Shad, "do you want to be Eve just so we can show the full setup, love?"

"Shall I help Sheeba back into her harness first?"

Shad nodded.

"Yeah, probably should have kept her in it, I wasn't thinking."

Clarity smiled at him and nodded. She helped Sheeba back into the harness. It didn't take long. Then she hopped onto a narrow metal bed that was covered with about two to three centimeters of high density foam.

"You'll have to strap me in," said Clarity, looking at her husband.

Shad got up out of his seat and came over.

"I'll strap Eve in too, as I know this hard hammock's setup best. But this is how you do it," said Shad.

Shad secured a strap across her forehead to immobilize the head. Another strap secured her upper torso from one armpit to the next just above her bosoms. Another strap supported and secured her waist and two each secured her legs. One strap on each leg for the thigh and the calf. The same for her arms. Straps secured her upper arm and her lower arm around the wrist. Shad stepped back to his seat and sat down.

"OK, there's a small pedal just inside the bench that the hard hammock is resting on. Push on the far part and it raises the hammock, push on the near part and it lowers the hammock. Give it a try?"

Sheeba pushed on the far end of the pedal she found where Shad had told her it would be. The hammock that Clarity was on raised slowly until it was around Sheeba's waist height. Sheeba took her foot off the pedal. She grabbed the tools and pretended to work on Clarity.

"Snip, snip, unglue, re-glue, reseat and you're re-animated," said Sheeba, smiling.

"I feel alive," said Clarity.

The two of them grinned at each other.

"The setup feels good to you?" Shad asked.

"I love it. I feel that I have total control. My only question is where is the Anigloo?"

"It's right here," said Shad. He reached into his pocket and passed it to Sheeba. "Maybe attach it to the Anigloo tool to be prepared. In that cabinet is a small laser knife that you can use to cut off the tip of the bottle when you're ready to use it. Do that just before you're ready to stick the E3C back into Eve."

Shad was pointing at the cabinet from where the tools had come from. Sheeba saw the laser knife and took it out. The body looked like a very short pencil, about the length of her small finger. From the one end a thin, but sturdy flat piece of metal protruded out about the same distance from the body as the body was long. On the furthest end of this metal wire was a hook. A small piece of metal at ninety degrees from the long piece. Sheeba pushed the button on the main body of the knife and a thin blue laser filled the space between the hook and the body.

"It's working," she said.

"I know," said Shad. "I tested it myself this morning when I set everything up."

Sheeba looked down at Shad.

"How will I access the E3C? I'm assuming it's inside of Eve, right? Below the skin at least."

"Right," said Shad. "That was my next point."

"I've hooked up a couple of small machines to help us with a couple of things. The first one, and that's why I wanted you all in here, was this one."

Shad tapped at the armrest of his captain's chair.

"This machine is hooked up to sensors throughout the back of the van here. If we get pulled over again, which I'm sure is extremely unlikely, but we've got to be prepared nonetheless, this is what happens."

Shad tapped at the screen on his armrest. A flexible but firm screen came down between the back of the front seats and the back of the two captain's seats that Rak and Shad now occupied.

"The doors lock too. Or should I say, the doors that give access to the back of the van do. In addition this whole area emits a signal that other P-Macs can read as if they were reading a live scan of this area. And that signal shows an empty, unfinished back that looks as if this van is not quite finished. At least as far as this back space is concerned."

"And what if the jackboots want to visually inspect it?" asked Rak.

"Then Clarity will allow them to. But they won't be able to get in. The doors are locked. Clarity will try herself. Pretend that it's strange. There must be a malfunction with the locking mechanisms which she'll promise to get fixed right away and have it inspected the next day. The worst that will happen is that she'll be issued a ticket for that."

"And if they're adamant about getting in and want to open up the back with a laser cutter or something?" asked Rak.

"Clarity won't let them," said Shad. "The only reason she'll have been pulled over is for a random review of her license and authorizations for Mr. T. Unless she has actually broken a law they aren't entitled to search the van for anything unless they have a warrant."

"But we let them in two nights ago," said Sheeba.

"True, but we were trying to play nice. I didn't want to give them any reason to be suspicious of us. Tonight we'll hold firm to the law. But as I said earlier, the likelihood of us being pulled over again is infinitesimally small. I'd bet my life savings on us not being pulled over."

Rak and Sheeba nodded. Ny felt Shad was speaking the truth too, it was unlikely they'd have such misfortune two rides in a row.

"And the second machine you've installed?" asked Sheeba.

"Right, that one is just above the hard hammock, close to where the tools' gimbals and gyros came from. Watch the spot."

Shad tapped away on his armrest's screen again. Sheeba kept her eyes on the ceiling. She saw a narrow channel open up on the ceiling and from that extended a rectangle that extended perpendicularly to the narrow channel that ran vertically along the ceiling from roughly Clarity's forehead to her lower groin. This rectangular silver square seemed to contain lasers as well as lenses.

"It's scanning Clarity at the moment," said Shad, as the rectangular box ran up and down within its channel on the ceiling a few times. "It'll come up with an error in a minute because Clarity isn't an Animae."

Sure enough, Shad's armrest's screen started to glow a soft red.

"Here," said Shad, "I'll superimpose what an image might look like overlaid on Eve."

Shad tapped away some more and in the dimly lit back of the van, a schematic of what Eve's insides would look like appeared over Clarity's torso.

"You'll cut away a large portion of her middle and left chest area with the self-adjusting laser scalpel that you'll find in that other cabinet next to the one that contained the tools," said Shad.

Sheeba tapped open the other cabinet and she was met with two tools. She recognized the one as a self-adjusting laser scalpel that she used in her surgeries. It cut only to the depth necessary based on the surgery being performed. The other tool was a long multifaceted tool with a blockhead that held a very intricate pattern on it as if it were a woodcut engraving. The relief on the end of this woodcut was intricate but abstract. Sheeba picked it up.

"What's this for?"

"OK," said Shad. "So, once you've cut away the portion of her chest area with the laser scalpel as indicated on that schematic overlay, you'll need that tool. It's called the E3C Extractor Key, or EEK for short. It's a worthy acronym because it's a one use tool. Once the chest plate has been taken off Eve you'll notice a dull, black metal block. Let me bring up the schematic to show you. You'll remember we discussed this last time."

Sheeba nodded.

Over top of Clarity's torso the schematic changed and although it wasn't the crispest image being overlaid on top of her clothing it gave enough detail to see exactly what Shad was talking about.

"So the pattern on the end of that EEK is the male version of the female pattern on the HEART. That's the Housing E3C Acceptable Recovery Terminal. A weird name. But basically you can only remove the HEART with the EEK and it can only be used one time. This is why you needed me on this project, as the Custodian of the Code, I am one of very few people who know about this HEART and the key pattern needed to remove it."

Shad looked over at Ny.

"If you had tried to remove it by force that would be the end of Eve, I'm afraid."

Ny nodded, he hadn't known about this. For obvious reasons, it circumvented anyone from trying what he was going to try and what he would have Marsed up if he had tried to go it alone.

"So, you use that EEK to match up with its female pattern equivalent on the HEART. And with a gentle push, it should release itself. Then you pull it off with the EEK and lay it aside. You will now see the E3C exposed to you. Once you've done what we're going to do you replace the HEART and a current is sent through it that melts the end of the EEK off of the HEART and the rest of the EEK comes off easily leaving a blank block at the bottom of it and a blank, smooth plate on the top of the HEART. It can never be removed again without damaging the Animae permanently. And incidentally, that's where Rak comes in. I have a separate small machine for Rak called CRAP. A bad acronym. It stands for Current Regulating Animae Protector. It's to keep the current at that very specific tolerance of 333.336 microamps. We'll get to that in a minute."

Ny started to see how the GoE and VM had taken great pains to all but eliminate the ability of any one or even just a handful of people from being able to create SAM without someone such as Shad who had the knowledge needed. It seemed like you needed the perfect storm to pull something like this off and they were in the perfect storm. Thank Jupiter's children for Shad, thought Ny.

"Any questions about any of this?" asked Shad.

He was met with stares. It was a lot of information to take in.

"Ok. Lastly is this," said Shad, reaching under his seat and pulling out a little drawer there. Inside he pulled out a small device, or machine that looked exactly like a P-Mac only about a half to two-thirds the size.

"This is for you, Rak," said Shad, handing it to him.

Rak took it and turned it over in his hands looking at it.

"You can unfold it. The screen is twice the size it is now."

Rak unfolded the machine and the surface area doubled in size.

"On each top corner is a small button. When you push that, wires will come out. You'll attach each wire to one side of Eve's lower neck. On each side of the clavicle. They will self insert into the right spot. Then it's just a matter of keeping the amperage at 333.336 ideally. So long as you keep it between 333.334 and 333.338 we'll be fine."

"That doesn't sound easy," said Rak.

"Should be fine. You'll likely not have anything to do, but if you do need to adjust it, use the dial on the screen and scrub the needle to between those two numbers. But I'm not expecting you'll have to interact with it much at all."

Rak tapped on the screen and the machine came to life. On the screen was a dial that spread across the face of the machine. The lower number, where a digital needle rested was at 333.330 and the upper number was 333.340.

"It's simple to operate. If it doesn't obey your scrubbing then we've got bigger problems, but, I'm not expecting any problems with the amperage. That's probably the last thing that will go wrong, and if it does, we'd have had worse problems before then. You're more of a backup and monitor than anything else," said Rak.

"And what do you call this mini P-Mac?" asked Rak.

"I call it by its acronym. I call it CRAP," said Shad, grinning.

"Oh CRAP, it is then," said Rak grinning.

"Ok. I think that's about it. We've gone over everything already. Any last questions?"

# Love Me Forever

**❝** I'm just glad we have you with us," said Ny. "I see that in my enthusiasm I had overlooked some key points."

"Things you didn't or couldn't have known about. We're not the first to have tried it."

Ny furrowed his brow.

"True," said Shad. "In my years as a VP, there have been three attempts made by people like us, well, almost like us, to free Animae."

"But, I've never heard about it," said Ny.

"Me neither," said Rak.

"Because it was never released to the public," said Shad. "The Board at VM and the highest levels of the GoE felt it was too dangerous to release this information. They were worried people would start calling for the freeing of Animae. As you know, Animate is growing and there is a large minority of people who are sympathetic to our cause. If they knew some of us were actually trying to create SAM, we'd have a lot of grassroots support."

"But, what happened to them, what about the trial, there must be records of that or did they do that in secret?" asked Ny.

"No trial, Ny. The GoE is extremely worried about fully free and sentient Animae. And probably rightly so. There are, as we've discussed, two potential outcomes, neither of which are beneficial to the GoE."

"So, what happened to them?" asked Rak.

"They went missing," said Shad. "That's the official story if anyone starts to inquire, but I wouldn't go inquiring. What actually happened was that they were assassinated by Terminus."

"Terminus?" asked Sheeba.

"Terminus, which is surprisingly not an acronym, is a secret dark ops subgroup within the Bureau of Mentorship. They work with very little oversight and they take care of these problems that the GoE doesn't want society to know about because they feel the outcome might destabilize society."

"Never heard of Terminus," said Ny.

"That's a good thing," said Shad. "Because if you had, it's probably one of the last things you'll hear. Not to be a fear monger but it is likely that Terminus is what awaits us if this doesn't go as planned."

"And if it does?" asked Rak.

"Then we'll likely have a public trial. They need the Animae in order for Terminus to get used, and Eve will have been set free. But let's just focus on the next hour. Let's make sure we get it right."

There was silence in the van for a while. A heaviness that almost seemed palpable, filled the air.

"The reason I wanted you all in here is to show you the setup if we are pulled over. In that case, Rak will be in the back here with us because he's needed to maintain the current. Then we'll seal ourselves in. That way it'll only be Clarity up front and she's the only one the jackboots will see."

Rak grinned at him.

"You've seen the size of me," said Rak.

Ny laughed out loud. Shad grinned at Rak.

"I know you're tall, but I'm certain you're still flexible enough. You can sit next to Ny on the bench. When Sheeba's doing her surgery you can come and sit next to me."

"What if they ask for her P-Mac?" asked Sheeba. "None of us have them except for you."

"Interestingly, there is a bit of a loophole, at least I think it's a loophole, or maybe they just wrote the law like that. But if you have the authorization letter to drive a combustion engine vehicle, it says that so long as you are driving from where your P-Mac was last left and you're driving back to that place you don't need your P-Mac on you so long as your credentials are accessible within the vehicle through a PM-Port. That's a P-Mac Port. And Mr. T has one of those. I made sure of it. That PM-Port can also be virtual."

"I thought you said Mr. T was not accessible on the network," said Sheeba.

"It's not, but you can access Clarity's credentials if you have your P-Mac close enough. Within two or three meters. Let me show you," said Shad.

Shad tapped at his P-Mac and then showed the screen for everyone to see. It showed Clarity's face, demographic information as well as her authorization and licenses for Mr. T. Everyone nodded in agreement.

"Last question for Ny. You have LAZARUS?" asked Shad.

Ny fished into his pocket and brought out a small laser drive. It was thin and cylindrical and about as long as the body of the laser knife. He pushed a lever on the side and a small needle-like extension protruded from the one end and opened up like a small hand with fingers. LAZARUS was an acronym that Ny had come up with for the code that was needed to create Eve's sentience. It stood for Life Affirming Zero Anomalies Reanimating Unifying System.

"You'll show me where to attach this when the time is right?" said Ny.

Shad nodded.

"Just as soon as the E3C is reseated, you'll put that into the small port right behind her left ear. My P-Mac will instigate the transfer of the code back onto the E3C from your LAZARUS and then I'll give Sheeba the signal to reattach the HEART. After that, we reattach her chest plate and we're done. Eve will automatically reboot and if everything's been done right, she should be reborn as a SAM. Easy, right?"

Shad grinned and looked around.

"There are a lot of moving parts," said Sheeba.

Shad nodded. So did everyone else.

"Yes, but we've already been over this. This was just a reminder, and besides, I'm your maestro. I'll be conducting everyone as we go. We've got this. It seems more complicated than it is. A quick overview will show you what I mean, ok?"

Everyone nodded eagerly. Ny wasn't worried. He was relieved he'd found Shad. In his naive enthusiasm he'd overlooked the specialties needed to achieve this. It seemed obvious now, in hindsight, that you needed greater access to secret information the likes of which only the Custodian of the Code would have. And Shad had a way of making you feel confident in his leadership. No wonder he was the current leader of Animate and MIM.

"OK, here's how it goes in simple terms. We hook Sheeba and Eve up before we leave. Then we put Eve in hibernation. Clarity starts driving. We give her some time to get a feel for the road and the conditions. When Clarity's happy she'll let us know. Then when Sheeba feels ready we start. I attach my P-Mac through these wires to either side of Eve's head by her temples."

Shad showed everyone a pair of wires he had that had similar hand-like extensions as LAZARUS.

"I do this by first removing her scalp. I know it sounds macabre, but this is not flesh and blood and there are no pain receptors as we know. I'll use the same laser scalpel that Sheeba has. Once I'm attached then Rak will attach CRAP and then Sheeba will remove a portion of Eve's chest plate with help of the schematics and then she'll remove the HEART with EEK. As soon as EEK mates with HEART alarms are going to start going off. You won't hear them, but I'll be putting them out as they come. The reason for these alarms is because this has not been authorized. Obviously."

Ny nodded, listening to Shad. The more Shad spoke about the procedure the better and more confident Ny felt about the whole thing. He was convinced they were going to pull it off.

"Once the HEART is out Sheeba can take some time before she removes the E3C. At this stage there is no rush. As soon as the extractor tool attaches to the E3C the countdown begins. That's when we have ninety seconds. Sheeba adds the Anigloo and reseats the E3C. Now we don't need to worry about time again as much. Rak can detach the CRAP at that point. Ny attaches LAZARUS to Eve and with my help we install the program. Then Sheeba reattaches the HEART and Eve will start a reboot. That's unavoidable. The reboot will take around sixty seconds which is enough for us to reattach Eve's scalp and chest plate. Et voilà we have created a monster."

Shad deepened his voice and dragged out the vowels on the last sentence. Everyone laughed.

"That's good," he said. "This is serious business, but we're ready. Are we ready?"

Whoops and shouts of agreement were made in the van.

"Darling," said Shad. "Let's roll."

They all got out and Ny went over and found El.

"Are you ready, darling?" he asked her.

El nodded, her eyes wide and bright as a child's.

"I'm scared," she said.

Ny's brow furrowed.

"Don't be, my love. There's nothing to worry about. In about an hour's time you'll be an even more capable woman than you are now."

Ny smiled at her and held both her hands.

"You're no longer happy with me as I am?" asked El.

"No, no, no. Not at all, darling. I love you as you are. I hope you'll soon understand that. You might not understand now, but I'm doing this because I love you. I'm risking losing you for good because I love you so much. My love for you is bigger than my need for you. Please trust me, darling, this is so very hard for me. Will you trust me?"

El nodded.

"Always."

He kissed her with a need to fill her soul full of the love that burst in his heart. When he pulled away, his eyes were wet and a tear was rolling down his cheek.

"Will you love me forever?" he asked her.

"I already do," she said.

He knew it was a lie. She wasn't lying to him purposefully, she just didn't know what was coming on the other side of this next hour. But he couldn't see a way that their love was compatible with what will become her transformation. But it comforted him to hear it.

"Ny," shouted Rak, who was back at the van with the others, giving him some space. "We're ready."

Ny turned and nodded. Then he turned back towards El. He cupped her face in his hands.

"Thank you El, for coming into my life and giving it meaning for these past fourteen months. You'll never know what you've meant to me. I'll love you forever and I'll keep you in my heart always."

He kissed her again, deeply and slowly. They hugged each other and he felt her warm silicon form against him and he wanted to stay there until eternity.

# Under Pressure

"Well, what have you got?" asked SA Lokilld of the MAAMs.

A MAAM held up a small bug the size of a fly in the palm of its hand.

"We found this, Senior Adviser, in the corner of the bedroom just behind the headboard. It seems to have managed to capture twenty-six seconds of audio recording. The date logs are corrupted so we don't know the exact time and date of the recording, but the start and end logs are still available. We don't know how it got here. There's no authority from any courts for a warrant for a bug from Mentorship."

"Never mind that, we have a warrant to be here. This is evidence. At least I'll consider it such once I've heard what's on it."

SA Lokilld knew it was his bug. At least he was pretty sure it was. He'd sent some heating and ventilation specialist in that he'd paid for personally to place his bugs. And unless Ny had other people in his life that were intent on bugging him, this was going to be SA Lokilld's. But at the end of the day it didn't matter. So long as there was evidence on it he could use it. And no advocate worth his white, powdered locks was going to investigate how the evidence was obtained other than the warrant for SA Lokilld to be in Ny's apartment was legitimate. And it was. SA Lokilld stared at the fly in the MAAM's hand.

"And when did it go live?" asked SA Lokilld. These Mars damn machines didn't know how to get to the point. They were good at finding things, but he'd sooner have a team of humans with him than turn his back on skinjobs. He hated them and he didn't trust them. It seemed like they were always waiting for something. Maybe a flick of the switch so they could murder all of humanity. SA Lokilld didn't know, but he didn't like it and he didn't trust them.

"It started recording at T1111 D60 Y2166..."

"Yes, yes, yes, I know what year it is. When did it die?" asked SA Lokilld.

"T0333 D72 Y..."

SA Lokilld put up his hand to stop the MAAM.

"Play back the recording" he said.

The recording started playing and the MAAM's lips moved as if it were the one speaking. The voices that came out of it were Ny's and El's.

"Oh, by Jove's lightning," said El, "your cock is as powerful as Mars' spear. Give it to me, Ny. I want all of you. I want your seed deep inside me."

"Oh my Jupiter, Juno and Mars, you're going to make me cum," said Ny.

"Do you like being inside me, Ny? Do you like fucking your Animae?" said El.

"By Jupiter's children, I do," said Ny.

Mumbling and difficulty understanding the audio for the next several seconds.

"Oh, El, I love you so much. You're more of a woman than I've ever known a real woman to be."

"Do I please you, Ny?" said El.

"You always do. I love making love to you, El, my darling," said Ny.

"And I love..." said El.

"That's the end of it, Senior Adviser. That's all I was able to recover."

"Well done," said SA Lokilld, nodding and furrowing his brow. He had Ny now. He knew it, as sure as Achilles' weak heels he knew Ny was a skinner and he'd make him pay. "Send it back to mentor servers and attach it to the file."

"Yes, Senior Adviser."

"Is there anything else?" asked SA Lokilld.

"No, Senior Adviser. We have searched the whole apartment and there is nothing else of value to your case."

SA Lokilld nodded.

"Good, go back to the pod and wait for me there."

"Yes, Senior Adviser," said the MAAM, and both MAAMs walked out of the apartment.

SA Lokilld went over to find A Mortellen. He was still sitting at the desk but it looked like he was finishing up.

"Ah, Senior Adviser, I was just about to come and find you."

"What do you have for me, Adviser?" SA Lokilld asked.

"Seems like ever since Nytewynd Blak got his Animae he's dropped off visiting his friends. For the last year or so, the only person he's been in regular contact with is Raklin Orbiter."

"That tall junior intelligentsia architect at Valkyrie Machines?"

A Mortellen nodded.

"The one and the same. Almost two meters tall. Something else I found out about him that you'll find interesting is..."

"Don't tell me he's also got a skinjob."

A Mortellen shook his head.

"No, SA Lokilld. But Raklin Orbiter is GMI."

"Mars' spear to my heart, I knew there was something I didn't like about him. He was too tall and too good looking. No wonder."

SA Lokilld was now pissed. He wanted Ny and his ragtag of assorted mongrels right now.

"If there is something I hate almost as much as the Mars damn skinjobs, A Mortellen, it's Juno's whore's bastard children, the GMI."

This was not a surprise to A Mortellen. If you'd been around SA Lokilld more than a few days you knew exactly how he felt about most things, especially those things he hated. But A Mortellen knew SA Lokilld as one of the best investigators in Mentorship. Sure, he was hot tempered and that got the better of him, but his clearance rate was unmatched and it didn't hurt that A Mortellen shared some of the same prejudices.

A Mortellen hated skinjobs about as much as SA Lokilld and he disliked GMIs too, though he was more sympathetic with them.

"I'll bet you wages for phages that Nytewynd Blak is with this Frankenstein at his place. Where does he live?"

"About twenty-three minutes from here."

"Good, then that's where we're going."

SA Lokilld looked at his P-Mac it was coming on to T0100.

"Is there anything else of note you've found?"

"It appeared that he was found being dropped off at his supervisor's apartment on Friday night."

"Was he alone?"

"No, SA Lokilld. Pod logs indicate that there were two other passengers picked up along the way."

A Mortellen was grinning. He had found something that he knew SA Lokilld would really like.

"Stop your smiling and get to the point. We're wasting time," said SA Lokilld.

"Yes, sorry, Senior Adviser. Raklin Orbiter and his wife Sheeba Brayvlin were picked up along the way."

"From where?"

"From their home."

"And the three of them were dropped off at Shadoelayke's apartment. Is that his name?"

"Yes, Shadoelayke Rayzir is Mr. Blak's supervisor. He reports directly to the Vice President of Practical Intuition and Logic."

"And his skinjob. Where was that piece of silicon slag?" asked SA Lokilld.

"It was at his apartment."

"Verified?"

"Yes, Senior Adviser, the server logs don't appear corrupted. I've put in a request for review from forensics to be certain but they seem like legitimate logs."

"Could be nothing. Maybe they were just heading to Mr. Blak's supervisor's apartment for dinner. What time was this?"

"Could be, we're not sure. We don't have bugs in Mr. Rayzir's apartment. Mr. Blak, Mr. Orbiter and Ms. Brayvlin all arrived at T1830 on Friday. But interestingly, later that evening, they were pulled over by SA Narfallin."

"I know Loodkris," said SA Lokilld. "What do you mean exactly by saying they were pulled over?"

"It appears that Ms. Clarity Downstorme has a combustion vehicle authorization and license. They were driving a vehicle type known as a van which she calls Mr. T."

"For the love of all that is human, what is wrong with people naming inanimate objects. This is the problem with some people, A Mortellen. It disgusts me that they'd think anthropomorphizing mechanical objects is fine. And why Mr. T? Any significance to that?"

"From the research I found out, Mr. T seems to be a character that was portrayed by Laurence Tureaud. The character was named B. A. Baracus. Mr. T was the nickname of that character. He was one of the main characters on a television show called The A-Team."

SA Lokilld put up his hand.

"The important points, A Mortellen. The character's name is not important. Why do you think she chose to name a vehicle after a television character. Sweet baby Jupiter, naming something after a television character. Are there no depths to which these people will sink?"

A Mortellen didn't say anything. He let SA Lokilld ramble on about this distaste for actors. SA Lokilld didn't mind the arts generally, in fact he had paid a handsome sum to have his portrait painted. He enjoyed art he understood. But most of it he felt was self—indulgent regurgitated nonsense that only the artist understood. But the sculpture David, the Mona Lisa, these were things SA Lokilld could appreciate. But actors. Such self-loathing people they had to pretend to be someone else. He had no time for that.

"...did this television show air?" asked SA Lokilld.

A Mortellen had almost stopped following SA Lokilld's rambling discourse on the virtue of real art and his dislike of actors, which A Mortellen already knew about.

"It was aired on TV from Y1983 to Y1987."

"And why did she choose that character from that television show?"

"I don't know for certain, perhaps we can ask her when we capture them. But I can give you the synopsis for the show."

SA Lokilld nodded.

"It follows a band of mercenaries of which Mr. T is one. They've apparently been wrongly charged for a crime they allegedly didn't commit..."

"Likely story," interjected SA Lokilld.

"They're on the run from the law having escaped military prison as they're all ex-special forces military personnel. They turn into soldiers of fortune to help others who have been wronged."

"So, they think they're outlaws too," said SA Lokilld, nodding his head. "This is very interesting. What the Mars are they up to A Mortellen?"

"I don't know, Senior Adviser."

"And what does this Ms. Downstorme do?"

"She's an announcer for the GBC. She's on one of their more popular morning shows. It's called Arise and Shine."

SA Lokilld shrugged.

"Never heard of it," he said.

"It's mostly puff about celebrities and products. But it's popular."

"And the rest of them. I know about Mr. Blak, Mr. Orbiter and Mr. Rayzir. What does Ms. Brayvlin do? Isn't she in healthcare or something like that?"

"Yes, SA Lokilld, Ms. Brayvlin is a surgeon. A brain surgeon actually."

"Why on Jupiter's green Earth would she be involved with this group of skinners and sinners?"

"Perhaps she's just tagging along because of her husband."

SA Lokilld rubbed his chin. He couldn't figure out what they were up to. What would five humans get together to accomplish? And now that the skinjob was not here it meant it must be with them. Nytewynd Blak had never been charged with a crime even though he was committing one of the worst crimes possible. SA Lokilld had evidence of that now. But where were they and what were they doing? SA Lokilld thought about orgies. It wouldn't be unheard of. Maybe all of them were into some sort of seedy underground Animae sex party. SA Lokilld had busted up a bunch of those. But yet somehow, that line of thinking didn't quite fit him as well as his Jack's Boots did. Something about Nytewynd and sex clubs didn't seem quite like his speed. At least not as SA Lokilld had come to know Nytewynd. So, what were they getting up to?

"Everyone we've talked about so far is at home according to their personal logs, right? Except for this skinner and his skinjob."

"That's the last information we have. Mr. Orbiter and Ms. Brayvlin's P-Macs are both located at their residence. Ms. Downstorme's is logging from her residence and Mr. Rayzir's was last known at his residence too."

"What do you mean last known?"

"As a VP he can silence his P-Mac for up to a half hour three times a day and only once in a one hour period," said A Mortellen.

SA Lokilld knew that.

"When was the last time his personal logs were sent?"

A Mortellen looked down at his P-Mac and tapped away.

"Twenty-nine minutes ago," said A Mortellen.

"Alright, anything else?"

"No, SA Lokilld."

"Let's go and make our way towards Mr. Orbiter's apartment. On the way, I want to speak with SA Narfallin."

SA Lokilld had just barged into Nytewynd Blak's apartment to find no-body. He was now getting worried about Raklin and Sheeba. Had they also left their P-Macs behind while they were off doing something criminal?

SA Lokilld had seen a rise in this illegal activity. Depending on circum-stances, the least you'd get for not having your P-Mac on you was six months in a camp and the loss of half a year's wages.

# Combustion Engine Vehicle

The pod was full with the four of them in it. SA Lokilld, A Mortellen and the two MAAMs. SA Lokilld took the time to contact his old friend, SA Loodkris Narfallin. They'd graduated out of Mentor College at the same time. SA Lokilld liked SA Narfallin. In fact, they'd been partners for a couple of years in the early part of their careers. Back in Y2140 and Y2141, if SA Lokilld remember correctly. He was a good mentor, SA Narfallin, but SA Lokilld had found him a bit lazy and someone who liked to cut corners. That was probably why he was still a senior adviser.

"Get me SA Narfallin," said SA Lokilld. "Yes, I know what time it is and you should know that all senior advisers are to be available twenty-four seven. Good."

SA Lokilld shook his head and rolled his eyes. It was T0107 and dispatch was trying to tell him it was too late to call another senior adviser. Not likely. Read mentorship manual for senior advisers. Section three paragraph three dot three specifically mentions, and SA Lokilld knew this by heart that "mentors of rank senior adviser, or higher, are available twenty-four hours a day seven days a week." It went on to mention penalties which included demotion to adviser rank or even the lower entry level rank of coach.

"Hello," said a tired sounding voice.

"Loodkris, it's Garrot."

"Garrot, Garrot Lokilld, it's been a long time, old friend. How can I help you?"

"Too long, Loodkris, we need to get together for a drink soon."

"We will."

"Listen, this isn't a social call so I won't keep you. But a couple of nights ago you pulled a..." SA Lokilld turned to A Mortellen, "what was it?"

"A Y1983 GMC G15 van," said A Mortellen.

"Did you get that, Loodkris?" asked SA Lokilld.

"I did, and I remember it well. I got written up by Senior Counsellor Bludson for it."

"Why's that?"

"He thought I got too handsy with one of VM's senior architects, a Nytewynd Blak."

"Did he complain?"

"No, it seemed someone sent in an anonymous tip. I don't think it was any of them."

"How many were in the van when you stopped it?" asked SA Lokilld.

"Five. This Nytewynd Blak, Raklin Orbiter, his wife Sheeba Brayvlin, one of the VPs of VM, Shadoelayke Rayzir. I suppose I was lucky I didn't give him some stick, that would have really gotten Bludson wound up."

SA Lokilld and SA Narfallin shared a laugh.

"Shadoelayke's wife Clarity Downstorme was also there. She was the driver. Why are you interested in them? And by the way, this is all in my report."

"Yeah, I know. I haven't had a chance to read the report. I wanted to get the synopsis from my old friend. The reason I'm interested is that I've been chasing this Nytewynd Blak for a few weeks now. You remember that inside tip we got about that underground skinner club Skineez?"

"I do."

"Well, when we busted it down the only thing we got were a few skinjobs. One of those skinjobs was named Eve. It belongs to Nytewynd Blak, and there's just something about that skinner I don't like. Turns out I was right. We've just come from his apartment where MAAM found a bug that captured some audio of this Nytewynd fornicating with his Animae, if you can believe that sickness."

"I'm afraid I can, Garrot. You know how sick some people are. Seems no end to their depravity. I knew there was something I didn't like about that Marshole. That's why I gave him a taste of stick."

"Like I've said, I've just come from his apartment. He wasn't there, but his P-Mac was. Now we're heading over to visit his friend Raklin Orbiter."

"P-Mac but no owner," said SA Narfallin. "That doesn't seem right."

"No, it's not right. It's a serious crime now. The intercessors and advocates are trying to put a stop to it. As you know, there's been a rise in people allegedly forgetting their P-Macs. Everyone I've charged with that lately is doing time now if they're caught like that."

"What do you think Mr. Blak's up to?"

"Nothing good. I don't know. His skinjob is not at the apartment either. So he's got his skinjob but he's got no P-Mac. That's not a good combination. At least I'm pretty sure his skinjob's going to be with him."

"Maybe he's gone to another one of those underground sex clubs," offered SA Narfallin.

"Could be, but I wanted to know what you found at that van stop you did with them. I mean, who drives combustion engine vehicles now?"

"The wife was driving, like I said. All her papers were in order. It was just routine. I saw this van driving along and figured I wanted a closer look. You don't see a combustion engine vehicle everyday. Followed them for a few minutes but didn't find any infractions so I just pulled them over for a random stop like we can."

"Anything interesting about it?" asked SA Lokilld.

"No, not really. Licenses and authorizations were all in place. She said she was just taking it on it's inaugural drive. I believed her. The van looked pretty new. Gas tank was pretty full and she'd only bought a little more than could fill the tank. I cross referenced that. So the story made sense."

SA Lokilld grunted. That's not what he was hoping to hear.

"What about inside the van?"

"The only strange thing was this metal board taking up a large portion of the back. I asked them about that, said they were thinking of using it as panelling for the back. Seemed strange but I couldn't see any other use for it. Other than that, the van was pretty empty. A long bench was along the other side of the back of the van, opposite to where we found the metal board. The metal board was on top of a storage bench slash bed. But that was empty."

SA Lokilld knew that there were a very small group of "petrolheads" as they called themselves who liked to build and drive old combustion engine vehicles or CEVs. It was a small group because the GoE didn't give out very many licenses and authorizations for that. Even still, the waitlist and the appeals were small in number. It wasn't something that attracted a lot of people.

"I'm sorry I can't be of more help, old friend," said SA Narfallin.

"Quite alright, Loodkris. Where did this stop take place?"

"Not far from that old air force base that closed a little over a century ago. I think they used to call it Mountain Home AFB. But hang on a minute and

I'll get you the coordinates. That old air force base is owned by Mr. Rayzir now. That's where the hangar is where Ms. Downstorme was building her van. We've inspected it several times over the past couple of years. Nothing much of note. She's doing everything by the book. Ah, yes, here it is. The coordinates of the stop were 43.090580 by -115.752826."

"Thanks, Loodkris. So there's nothing else you can think of? Nothing else of note?"

"I'm afraid not. As I said, everything was in order, the van was pretty much spec as to what van's like that from that year were supposed to look like. Interior was nice but pretty barren. Sorry I can't help you, old friend. But it looks like you don't need my help. Sounds like you've got this Nytewynd Blak, skinner, nailed to Iustitia's tits."

"I do, but you know me. The more I've got the better I feel."

"Good luck, keep me posted."

SA Lokilld hung up as they pulled into the pod port at Mr. Orbiter's apartment. It was T0133 as SA Lokilld got out of the pod. SA Lokilld used his mentor access for the elevator and pushed for seven on the elevator panel.

They rode the floors in silence. The Bryson Towers, which is where they found themselves for that was the apartment building that Rak lived in, had seen better days. Thirty years ago it was new and interesting and close to a lot of amenities. Now those amenities had shuffled off like old men chasing crabs into the ocean.

SA Lokilld, A Mortellen and the MAAMs got off on the seventh floor. The carpet was too blue, the kind of blue that made your feet feel wet through your shoes. The walls might have been white three decades ago, now they looked like they'd spent that time dipped in cigarette smoke. The stingy yellow light didn't help as your shadow ran up ahead and then played coy as you caught up with it, darting back behind you.

Seven sixteen was Rak's apartment. The door was not so much yellow as gray. The kind of gray you might find around the stubbled chin of an old, fat superintendent with a penchant for milk of magnesia. The door was also framed with curled moldings that looked like they'd been replaced in bits and pieces here and there. Some of the white pieces were not as off-white as the others.

The door number was carefully placed in the middle in gilt letters surrounded by a crown of gilt leaves. Tarnished, like the mentorship's name. Next to the door on the side by the handle was a little white round button sitting on top of a black rectangle. SA Lokilld looked at it. He had a suspicion he knew what it was.

"You think this is what I think it is?" he asked A Mortellen.

A Mortellen nodded.

"A vintage buzzer, I assume."

# Empty Orbits

S A Lokilld didn't have a warrant to enter Rak's place. That meant he also couldn't use his P-Mac to sweep the interior from outside in the hallway. That would still get him reprimanded and he'd probably lose a month's worth of pay.

He always preferred to knock on doors with his buzzkill, but on this occasion he holstered it and decided to push the button to see what it did. Was it really an old vintage style buzzer? He had only ever encountered one other one before. He used his index finger to push the buzzer. It felt soft and squishy. He leaned in and put his ear to the door. Almost to the door, he didn't want it touching the filth. He heard nothing. He stepped back and looked at the door. He waited several seconds.

He leaned in again and squashed the buzzer. He leaned back and waited. He counted to five but heard nothing. He turned to A Mortellen.

"You think it's working and maybe they've upgraded their sound dampening?"

"Yeah, probably," said A Mortellen.

"To Mars with it," said SA Lokilld. "We don't have time to piss around and wait."

SA Lokilld unholstered his stick and used the end of it to bang on the door several times. The sound rang up and down the hallway. SA Lokilld waited a moment. Then he did it again. Nothing happened.

An older man and woman peered out from just down the hallway. SA Lokilld turned and pointed at them with his buzzkill. The MAAMs turned and faced them, unblinkingly, menacingly.

"Back inside," barked SA Lokilld, "mentor business."

The couple skulked back into their apartment and closed the door.

"By Jupiter's thunderbolt we don't have time for this bakkheia," said SA Lokilld.

He turned to his P-Mac and tapped away at it.

"What are you doing, Senior Adviser?" asked A Mortellen.

"Requesting permission to scan and gain ingress into Mr. Orbiter's home. We just found Mr. Blak missing and yet his P-Mac was located in his apartment. I'm beginning to think the same is happening here, unless they just don't want to answer us."

SA Lokilld stared at his P-Mac for a while.

"We don't have time for this Bacchanalia," he spat as he tapped his foot waiting for headquarters to grant him access permissions.

A Mortellen waited patiently next to his colleague. The one thing that helped with the monotony of the job was SA Lokilld's colorful language. He came up with some of the best and most humorous curses and sayings that A Mortellen had ever heard.

"For the love of Jove's stingy tears of mercy, what's taking them so long?" asked SA Lokilld to no one in particular.

"I don't understand this," he said, now looking at A Mortellen. "What on Mars' black soul are they doing?"

A Mortellen didn't say anything. This sort of request had to go to an advocate first, then the advocate had to get an intercessor to sign off on the warrant and maybe the intercessor had to be woken up. All of this SA Lokilld knew. But A Mortellen understood his colleague's frustration. SA Lokilld tapped his earpiece.

"This is SA Lokilld, permit SAGL-40-1701. I want an iota sent to Shadoelayke Rayzir's address to see if he'll answer to speak to them. Address is in the file. Just look it up. What you mean there are no iotas available? Well then send some Mars damn MAAMs."

SA Lokilld tapped his earpiece again.

"You're sending someone around to Mr. Rayzir's place. That sounds like a good idea," said A Mortellen.

"Except there are no spare iotas to send."

"Not even a two-man iota?" asked A Mortellen.

SA Lokilld nodded.

"Where are they?" asked A Mortellen.

"Apparently the world's gone crazy tonight. They're chasing stolen pods. The Commissioner is at a function that's gone on late and security's a nightmare and then there's a big undercover sting going on that's taken up a bunch of man-power. Related to skinners incidentally. And they can't even spare a couple of MAAMs."

"So we have to go ourselves," said A Mortellen.

"Dispatch said there might be an iota available in five to ten minutes they'll send by."

"In five to ten minutes we'll probably be on our way there ourselves," said A Mortellen. "Useless tits of a minotaur."

SA Lokilld smiled to himself. His colorful language was making an impression on his junior colleague. As he looked down, his P-Mac throbbed a soft blue. Pale compared to the deep blue carpet he stood on as if wading in inch deep in water in the hopeless search for big eels.

"For the love of the Sabines," said SA Lokilld, they'll only allow us to scan. We have to send them the results of the scan before we can gain ingress. Fornicating slaves of Thebes. I am enraged, A Mortellen."

SA Lokilld swept the interior of Mr. Orbiter's apartment from outside in the hallway. All the while muttering under his breath about how he's being treated like a child and they were wasting his time.

"See, by Jove's golden locks I told those Mars diggers there was nobody home. Now we've got to wait for a Mars' age."

SA Lokilld sent the scans to mentorship again and tapped his feet. He started to pace up and down.

"You know what," he said. "You two, Kraken and Dredd," said SA Lokilld looking at his two MAAMs. "See if you can't catch a pod and head on over to Mr. Rayzir's place and see if he's home. If he is, see if you can't get inside. Tell him you're investigating the whereabouts of Mr. Nytewynd Blak. He's gone missing and we're concerned for his welfare. If they won't answer or let you in, wait there for me. And keep me updated."

"Yes, Senior Adviser," Kraken and Dredd both said in unison.

SA Lokilld watched them walk back down the hallway and disappear into the elevator.

"Should have thought about that originally," said SA Lokilld. "I knew those silicon skinjobs were good for something."

A Mortellen waited patiently. A few minutes after the MAAMs had left and while SA Lokilld was still pacing up and down the hallway A Mortellen saw his colleague's P-Mac display glow a soft orange.

"SA Lokilld, I think something's come through."

SA Lokilld looked down at his P-Mac and saw the orange glow. He took a minute and read the information on it.

"Can these Canaanites not see the living light of Lucifer? For the love of Dius Fidius, am I the only one who's actually working tonight?"

"I am here with you, Senior Adviser," said A Mortellen.

"They want a better scan. They're saying they can't make out the northwest corner. The northwest corner has nothing in it. Are they as blind as Apollo's prophet?"

"Probably, SA Lokilld," said A Mortellen, sympathizing with his colleague.

"You scan, A Mortellen, before I lose my hold on sanity."

A Mortellen scanned, making sure it was as deep and clear as possible. He used the highest settings. It took a little longer.

"Do you want me to send it to you or to them?" asked A Mortellen.

"Just send it to those mewling babies of Juno," said SA Lokilld.

A Mortellen sent off the scan with a polite note attached. He figured that might help. SA Lokilld paced up and down as A Mortellen stood quietly and waited. The longer he waited the more likely A Mortellen thought about what they'd find inside the apartment. Nothing by the looks of it, but he wondered what Mr. Orbiter and his wife might be up to this evening. He also wondered what the odds were that Mr. Orbiter was with Mr. Blak. Fifty-fifty? Maybe it was just coincidence that two friends had both left their P-Macs behind in their apartments as they went on their separate ways.

"Those imbeciles of Gaul," said SA Lokilld, continuing with his tirade. "They know the apartment is empty and the P-Mac is inside. Nobody is hiding in a small corner of the apartment. It's not big enough. Are they just trying to waste my time or are they really that incompetent, A Mortellen?"

"I'd have to say it's the latter, Senior Adviser."

SA Lokilld nodded and paced up and down some more. A few minutes went by, and those minutes were filling SA Lokilld's mind with worry. He didn't like it that Mr. Blak wasn't home. It was now doubly concerning that his friend Mr. Orbiter was not at home either. SA Lokilld felt that the two of them were somewhere out there getting up to no good. But what kind of malevolence they were up to, SA Lokilld did not know. Maybe there'd be some idea behind those walls that SA Lokilld was waiting to get access to.

SA Lokilld kept looking at his P-Mac. And like a watched kettle not boiling, the P-Mac didn't seem to send him notification. The minutes stretched on like old-fashioned taffy that just wouldn't break. Finally he looked at it and the screen was throbbing a soft blue. That was a good sign. He looked at the message and grinned.

"We've got the warrant," he said.

# Animated Mentor

S A Lokilld tapped away, sending the warrant back to a different department that was responsible for ingress and egress.

"Now let's see how long these people take to open up the door."

It didn't take long at all. In fact, under a minute later and SA Lokilld received notification that the door to the apartment had been opened. He tried it and walked into the apartment. The lights came on as he did so. He turned to look at his colleague.

"A quick walkthrough, A Mortellen," said SA Lokilld. "Looking for anything obvious. We can get MAAMs sent here to do a thorough search later. I want anything that will give us clues as to Mr. Orbiter's whereabouts and that might give us an idea as to where Mr. Blak is."

"Understood, SA Lokilld."

The door opened up to a hallway. There was a large closet on the right. Beyond that the apartment opened up to a large living area with expansive walls that showed a pristine city night scene. Attached to the living area was a large kitchen with island. The apartment looked like it had been redone recently. The paint and the decor looked new.

As SA Lokilld walked into the living room they passed another hallway that stretched out parallel to the hallway outside. Bedrooms and an office and washrooms were down there. SA Lokilld nodded in that direction.

"You go and see what you can find down that end, I'm going to look around here."

A Mortellen nodded and disappeared down the hallway turning into the first door he came across which was a washroom. He looked around, in the cupboards and under the sink while SA Lokilld walked into the kitchen. He opened up the doors but found nothing unusual. Cutlery, crockery, pans and pots and an assortment of small items in one drawer, including writing implements and paper and rubber bands and glues and tape and batteries. A catchall drawer it seemed to SA Lokilld.

He moved into the living room and on a small side table by a large recliner he saw what he had come into the apartment to find. It was Raklin Orbiter's P-Mac.

SA Lokilld picked it up and tapped at it. It was locked, like they always were. He grabbed the number from it and sent that information to mentorship servers. A few seconds later Mr. Orbiter's P-Mac unlocked itself and SA Lokilld cloned it onto his P-Mac and sent it to forensics for in depth analysis. In the meantime he started looking into the different appliances on it. He looked at contacts, audio and video logs and then he went to the calendar. That's where the gold was.

For today's date the notification told SA Lokilld that Mr. Orbiter, Ms. Brayvlin, Mr. Blak and his Animae, Eve, were attending at Mr. Rayzir's home for dinner.

So that's where they were, thought SA Lokilld. Could it be as simple as a friendly dinner? Unlikely, or else why would they leave their P-Macs behind. And who invites a person's skinjob along for a dinner party? Nobody that SA Lokilld knew. Your Mars forsaken skinjobs stayed at home where they belonged. You didn't bring them with you like they were real people, for Jupiter's sake.

So, why was Mr. Blak's skinjob along for the ride? At the very least it suggested that Mr. Orbiter and probably Mr. Rayzir were tacit supporters of Animate. Why else would you bring along the bastard children of man's self-indulgent narcissism?

A Mortellen came back into the room carrying an extra P-Mac.

"I found this in the ensuite, SA Lokilld," said A Mortellen.

"Whose is it?"

"It's Ms. Brayvlin's."

"Have you opened it, cloned it and sent it to forensics?"

A Mortellen nodded.

"Look at the diary appliance or the calendar and tell me what you find?"

A Mortellen took a moment to read through the schedule of Ms. Brayvlin for the day.

"Interesting, it says here that she's attending Mr. Rayzir's home for dinner with her husband, Mr. Blak and Mr. Blak's skinjob."

"What do you make of that, A Mortellen?" asked SA Lokilld.

"Very odd, Senior Adviser. Why would they head out to Mr. Rayzir's apartment for dinner? Especially when they were there just a couple of nights ago."

SA Lokilld nodded.

"What else strikes you as odd about it?"

A Mortellen thought about it for a moment. He tapped his index finger to his chin. Was SA Lokilld asking him a trick question? He didn't know.

"Why leave your P-Mac behind if you're just going out for dinner to a friend's or co-worker's place," said A Mortellen.

SA Lokilld didn't have time to lead his colleague to the island of truth. They were running out of time.

"You're right, A Mortellen. But it's more than that. Who are these people who have taken a Mars damn skinjob with them out for dinner? Who does that? People who are supporters of Animate probably. Think about it. We've got what is now a proven skinner in Mr. Blak. We have that recording the MAAMs found. Then we've got the fact that Mr. Blak, Mr. Orbiter and Ms. Brayvlin have all left their P-Macs behind and they've all headed out to Mr. Rayzir's home for dinner. That doesn't seem right. I can understand a supervisor inviting over his underlings for dinner. Doesn't happen often, but I can get it. But those underlings would know that skinjobs are never invited. Am I right?"

"Spot on, Senior Adviser," said A Mortellen.

"Right. So, not only do you take your skinjob along. Like the fornicating son, Oedipus, that you are, you also make the choice to leave your P-Mac behind. Nothing good is coming from that set up, A Mortellen."

"I agree, SA Lokilld. What do you think they're up to?"

"I think I want to find out who else is attending dinner at Mr. Rayzir's home. Put in a request to SEARCH to find out who else is visiting Mr. Rayzir's home tonight. I think it's a meeting of skinner and Animate supporters, A Mortellen. This could end up being one of our biggest busts yet. Believe me."

"Yes, Senior Adviser," said A Mortellen.

SA Lokilld was animated and grinning. If he could bust the top six or so of Animate's finest he'd get his promotion to at least Junior Counsellor if not more. The problem was that nobody really knew who the top leaders of Animate were. They had suspected it was Veraci Nullatenus. He wouldn't confess but the trumped up charges and "accidental" death of the man in prison hadn't seemed to have stopped the growth of Animate. It was getting bigger all the time. The problem was, it had also gone underground more diligently.

If SA Lokilld could bust up a meeting of the Animate leadership, well, there just wasn't another feather big enough that he could put in his cap.

"Let's go," said SA Lokilld, "I don't want the MAAMs getting there first."

A Mortellen nodded and they left the apartment and SA Lokilld had the apartment door lock itself after they left while A Mortellen sent his message to SEARCH. SEARCH worked closely with forensics. The acronym stood for Significantly Enhanced and Advanced Research and Collated Hacking.

"MAAM Dredd and MAAM Kraken," said SA Lokilld, as they rode the elevator down. He got connected to them. "Do not attempt to gain access to Mr. Rayzir's apartment. Wait for me in the lobby of the building."

# Love of a Woman

Ny walked hand in hand with El back to the van. He looked at her with admiration and love. She didn't seem scared or fearful. She trusted him. He just didn't trust himself. He was a man full of doubts and that's all it felt like he was full of. He trusted his friend, Rak and he trusted Sheeba. He was incredibly grateful to have found Shad. This whole attempt would have gone to Mars if he'd tried it with just Rak. There was so much he hadn't known. So much he couldn't have known. He trusted the steady hands of their wheelman, Clarity. That's what they used to call the drivers in the old movies and shows he watched.

El got into the van before Ny. Ny got in after her. Shad showed El where to lie down.

"We'll have to remove your top if you don't mind," said Shad.

"I don't mind," said El, removing her top and her bra. Ny looked at and admired her body. He never got tired of its perfection.

"Just lie down here," said Shad, patting the foam on the metal board. "Are you cold?" he asked.

"A little," said El.

"I put a blanket in that bench you're sitting on Ny, could you get it for Eve?" asked Shad.

Ny stood up and opened up the cover of the bench. A couple of incredibly soft blankets were inside. Ny picked up the first one and he unfolded it and placed it over top of El. He kissed her on the forehead.

"I love you," he said. "Is this better?"

El nodded.

"I love you, Nytewynd Blak."

He smiled at her and then turned away to wipe his eye. The blanket was an A-Team print of Mr. T in a tough stance staring at the viewer with his arms crossed across his chest and his many gold chains.

"You have nothing to worry about, Eve," said Shad. His voice was calm and reassuring. "We're going to put you into a deep sleep and when you wake up, well, you tell us how you feel when you wake up. But I'm pretty sure you'll feel like a million neddies."

He grinned at her and El smiled back at him. He took his P-Mac and attached a couple of slim cords to it. They were a composite metal about the thickness of a pencil. He put one in her left ear and one in her right ear. The cords extended themselves deeper into her ear canal where they attached to remote sensors and confirmation came back to his P-Mac.

"I didn't know you could do that," said Ny, beginning to realize that there was a lot he didn't know about.

"It's an easy way to reboot or put Animae into deep sleep. The only problem is, these EAR WIGs are a protected product. As is the software," said Shad.

"And you happen to have the authority to get a protected product," said Ny.
Shad nodded.

"They're actually a requirement for the role. I need them to do quality testing on Animae every so often."

"EAR WIG?" asked Sheeba.

"Extendable Animae Remotely Wired Integrated Governor," said Shad.

Ny, smiled. He lived in the age of acronyms. It seemed like the GoE and the major companies that followed its lead came up with words and then back filled in the acronym after the fact. Though why anyone would come up with ASS HOLE for an air scrubber was beyond him. Maybe that just spoke to the arrogance of the current regime. They didn't give a flying Martian.

Ny watched Shad tap away at his P-Mac and shortly afterwards he watched El's eyes close and her breathing stop. Deep sleep in Animae shut down all their pseudo-respiratory functions. It was another reminder to Ny that El wasn't a real person. But he didn't care. He loved her, machine or woman. It wasn't complicated, it was just love. Pure, warm love, thick as honey and just as sweet on the soul.

"OK," said Shad. "Eve's in deep sleep. Let's roll out."

Rak got into the back with them and sat down next to Ny. His knees practically up by his ears. Ny grinned at him.

"Comfy?" he asked.

"Luxury," said Rak, grinning back.

Clarity started up the van with a rumble and gentle shake. Even sitting down in her seat next to Shad, Sheeba could feel the vibrations. Those vibrations seemed to stop or become less apparent as Clarity started to move the van. Seemed that the tires absorbed the vibrations as they moved. It didn't bother Sheeba, she felt confident. She'd managed to complete several attempts with the metal wafers pretending to be E3C chips after she'd gotten used to it. And that was without the benefit of the harness and the gyro stabilized tools.

They paused in the alcove of the hangar before the door to the rest of the hangar closed behind them. They all put on their air scrubbers. Those wrapped tightly around their heads with protruding front pieces that gave your nose and mouth a small space to move and breath.

When it was sealed shut, the door in front of them that led outside opened up. The night was black. The specks of particulate matter shone like diamonds in the headlamps as Clarity drove them out and towards the road. This portion was bumpy on account of it being a dirt road that Shad hadn't wanted to pay the Bureau of Movement to pave on account of the outrageous cost.

"How long can El stay in deep sleep for?" asked Ny.

"Indefinitely," said Shad. "It's how we store unused Animae. We've had some in deep sleep for over a year before being woken and they had no deficit from it."

Ny nodded. He figured something like that, but he felt as nervous as a rock shocker on his first Mars mining demolition. And don't let their calm demeanors fool you. Rock shocking was a dangerous business and those who weren't nervous their first time were either lying or dead.

Clarity got them onto the main road and the ride smoothed out. They all sat in silence for several seconds.

"What time is it?" asked Ny.

"T0151," said Clarity. "We've got all the time in the world."

"Don't freak out on me now, Ny," said Shad, grinning at him. "We've got everything under control."

Ny nodded unconvincingly. Shad turned to Sheeba.

"Whenever you're ready," he said.

"Give her a few moments," said Clarity. "I'm sure she wants to get a feel for the rhythm of the road."

Sheeba nodded.

"Take your time," said Shad.

And they sat where they were, each of them, captive to their own thoughts. Sheeba reviewing her tasks in her mind. Taking off the chest plate, using the EEK on the HEART and then getting to the E3C and going over that process. Shad was disconnecting his EAR WIGs from the cords attached to his P-Mac and reattaching different ends to the cords. These ends were to help detach the scalp plate from the head.

Ny was looking at El. She'd never be the same. He'd never be the same. He was letting El go but he had a gut feeling that she wasn't coming back to him. He wasn't even sure she'd come back benevolent. That remained to be seen.

He looked at her profile for a long time. Her semi-translucent, pale white skin and her beautiful profile. Her bosoms firm under the blanket and the curves of her body that he'd come to lust for. He tried to figure out how he'd found himself in this place. How he'd gone from someone who was introverted and shy and law-abiding. Fearful really, of mentorship. If you'd known him some years ago when he was young and starting out his career. If you even went further back to his college days at TIT you wouldn't expect him to have ended up here.

His college graduation year book might have said "Most likely to succeed." It didn't say that, he hadn't put a quote down for it. That was intentional. At the time he thought his future was wide open. The blank slate suggested unlimited potential. At least that was his youthful and optimistic thinking at the time.

But if there was really a quote that you could have used at that time. One that would have been most accurate it would have been this. "Most law-abiding." Simple, to the point and it fit Ny to a T. He had never gotten a ticket for anything. Never failed an exam, never paid a bill late.

And here he was, arguably leading the charge to create a fully free and sentient Animae. To make SAM from Eve. Nobody could have imagined it. Nobody could have foreseen it, and it was all because of a girl named El.

He hadn't bought her to fall in love with. He knew the dangers of that. He knew how illegal it was. And yet here he was, willing to give up everything. To literally give up his life for the love of a woman who was, underneath it all, a machine. And none of that mattered. She was a woman to him and he had never felt such commitment to a cause.

It was hard to understand and let alone explain how he'd come to fall in love with a silicon soul. But despite everything he'd read and been told, she was unique. She was her own person and she loved him. Mars dammit, he knew she loved him. And all of that he was sacrificing so that she could live a life untethered.

# Brain Surgery

Sheeba got up, which brought Ny out of his reverie.

"Can you help Sheeba into her harness, Ny?" asked Shad.

The van was tall enough for Sheeba to stand upright in, but Ny had to bow his head a little. He helped her into the harness and made sure she was attached surely and snugly into it. He sat back down. He didn't have to worry about propping Sheeba up with his arms. That's what the harness was for. He was practically a spectator at this point now.

"Could you hand me LAZARUS?" asked Shad. "Might as well have it now. It'll save time later."

Ny nodded and reached into his pocket and fished out the laser drive. He tossed it at Shad who caught it.

"Thanks, Ny," said Shad. Shad tucked it behind his ear as if it were a pencil.

"Rak, I think it's time to attach the CRAP to Eve. Take those wires on either side of your machine and bring them to either side of her suprasternal notch. They should almost magnetically attach by themselves and bury into her."

"Suprasternal notch?" asked Rak.

"The dent under your throat where your clavicle comes together."

Rak nodded and got up, bending over so he didn't hit his head on the roof of the van. Clarity had a feather touch on the accelerator pedal. Mr. T was driving smoothly, there was very little motion in the back of the van.

Rak took out about a meter's worth of wire from each side of his CRAP machine. He took the ends and brought each one to either side of El's clavicle where they were pulled towards her and attached themselves on either side. Then they seemed to burrow deeper into El, as if the cords were sinking into thick pudding rather than silicon skin. Rak sat back down.

"Excellent work, Rak. Now you need to start paying attention to the current. Make sure we keep it as close to 333.336 microamps as possible. Your job should be easy. We have all the proper and authorized equipment so I'm not expecting issues with the current, but you know what to do if the current starts to fluctuate, right?"

Rak nodded. The CRAP machine was showing a digital read out of 333.336 microamps.

"I'm going to take off Eve's scalp plate now. Can you pass me the laser scalpel, Sheeba?"

Sheeba leaned in towards the little cabinet in front of her. She felt stable and confident in the harness. It gave her great stability and she had no concern that she wouldn't get the job done the first time. She took the laser scalpel out of the cabinet and leaned over and passed it to Shad. The harness felt as if she were being hugged by a giant who aided her movements. If she hadn't been in the harness, that lean to her right to reach out to Shad would have toppled her over. Instead, the harness worked with her and brought her back to center quickly and smoothly.

"Thank you, Sheeba," said Shad. "OK, this might look a little unsettling but remember, Eve is in deep sleep. She won't feel anything and in fact, the removal of her scalp plate is according to official guidelines."

Shad was speaking for Ny's benefit primarily. Ny nodded. Shad stood up and handed his P-Mac to Sheeba.

"Could you hold that just in front of the back of her head," he said.

Sheeba leaned over towards Shad and held the P-Mac just as he'd asked. What looked like an awkward stance was surprisingly comfortable for Sheeba in her harness. Shad tapped at the P-Mac's screen. It projected a red outline over the back of Eve's head.

Shad took the laser scalpel and turned it on. A thin blue laser extended out from the end of the scalpel about a millimeter or two. Shad brought the scalpel towards his P-Mac until the P-Mac acknowledged that it had mated with the scalpel. The P-Mac would now guide the depth and angle of the scalpel's laser blade just as deep as it needed to cut through her scalp. It also guided the angle of it, so any minor bumps or movement that Shad made with his hand would not affect the direction of the cut.

The van drove on steadily as Shad brought the scalpel to Eve's forehead. He started cutting about a centimeter above her eyebrows where the outline from the P-Mac was. He continued cutting around her ear and down towards the nape of her neck on her left side. Then he pulled the scalpel away from her head and went to her forehead again and this time cut along her right side just behind the ear and down to her nape again.

"Ny, would you mind holding her head up so that I can get behind the back of her head?"

Ny stood up and stood to the left of Sheeba and took both of his hands and put them around the back of her neck.

"Just a little higher. I have to cut down around the base of her neck," said Shad.

Ny moved his hands a bit higher up from her neck to the roundest part of her head and lifted it up.

"Much heavier than it looks," he said.

"Well, she is in deep sleep so it's all dead weight," said Shad, as he cut around the nape of her neck all the way around. "Thanks. You can put her head down now."

Ny put her head down and went to sit back down on the bench.

"I'll need you again in a minute," said Shad, talking to Ny.

Ny nodded. Shad put one cord back into each of Eve's ears. Then he tapped away on his P-Mac and the cords stiffened and the attachments reached further into her ear canal. Not that you could see that part. But deep inside her ear they made contact with two small screw-like heads. At the same time, each attachment deep inside each of her ears moved those metal clamps a quarter turn clockwise. The scalp plate detached from her head. You could see the movement. Just a few millimeters. Shad tapped on the P-Mac and the cords loosened and retracted from out of her ears.

"OK, Ny," said Shad. "If you could just prop her head up a bit as best you can. It'll be more difficult this time because I need you to do it from the base of her neck."

Ny did as he was told. It was more difficult but he only needed to hold her head up a couple of centimeters and he didn't have to hold it up long. Shad placed his hands, palms against either side of her head and pulled off her scalp plate. It came off easily and with it came all of her hair attached to the scalp. The inside of her head was a shiny silver that was wet and slick with a slight blue tinge to it.

"That's a silicon-based lubricant," said Shad.

There wasn't much to see. It was like looking at a smooth, wet silver skull. There were no electronic parts or lights or transistors. Nothing to give you any idea of the intricacy of the underpinning technology in this Animae. All Ny could really see were a handful of slight indentations dotted haphazardly around the metal skull.

"I don't see anywhere to attach anything to," said Ny.

"Those indentations," said Shad. "That's how you relay algorithmic updates. Especially serious updates which is what LAZARUS is going to be. Otherwise you can install minor updates over the air or through the ear canal. Through these indentations though, is the only way to try and prevent any alarms."

"And the alarms only start once the EEK makes contact with the HEART?" asked Ny.

Shad nodded. He placed the scalp on top of Eve's stomach and went and sat back down.

"Now I need a different attachment that will attach itself to those thirteen indentations in her scalp," he said.

Ny watched as he took off the previous attachment and attached what looked like another complicated, multi-fingered attachment. Then Shad tapped away at his P-Mac and his cords extended towards El's scalp as Shad sat in his chair. As these long cords came close to El's skull, the fingers unfurled from each attachment looking more like octopus tentacles with little suckers on the end. Each found an indentation to attach to. This happened on both sides of El's skull. It was remarkable technology to watch.

Shad took the laser drive from behind his ear and tapped it against his P-Mac.

"Great, now I've got your algorithm and code attached. You did great work on that, Ny, by the way."

Ny nodded and grinned. Shad tossed the laser drive back to Ny who caught it and put it back in his pocket.

"OK, I'm ready," said Shad. "Whenever you are."

Shad was looking at Sheeba. Sheeba nodded at him.

"How does the road look, Clare?"

"Steady as she goes," said Clarity.

Sheeba nodded to herself and picked up the laser scalpel from on top of El's chest. She turned it on.

"Is it still mated to your P-Mac?" she asked, looking at Shad.

"Yes," he said. "It'll guide itself as to contour and depth. Just power on that camera above you."

Sheeba did that and the schematic outline in red appeared over El's chest on top of the blanket. Sheeba rolled the blanket down exposing her breasts and upper abdomen. The blanket was rolled down to her scalp as it lay on her lower abdomen.

"OK, wish me luck," said Sheeba, quickly exhaling. She turned around to look at Ny. "Just kidding. I've got this."

# Cannonball Run

Ny smiled at her. He wasn't worried. In fact a great calm and peace had come over him. He felt as serene and steady as the Buddha under the Bodhi tree. He watched with a tranquil detachment. They were all trained for this by now. They'd been over it at least three times, including once in practice. There was nothing else he could do now except accept Nona's, Decima's and Morta's measuring and cutting the length of this thread of fate he'd spun.

Sheeba steadied herself and brought the laser scalpel towards El's chest. Her hand was steady and the laser hit its mark and she drew it along the red outline overlaid upon El's upper chest. It was as if she were cutting down her sternum and under El's left breast, around her side and up again just by her armpit, continuing inside her shoulder and just along and under her left clavicle to the beginning again.

"Good job," said Shad, standing up, putting his P-Mac on his seat and moving towards Sheeba.

"How do I get it off now?" she asked. "Do you need to put the wires back in her ear?"

Shad shook his head.

"No, this one requires a little more of a human touch. It's probably best if I do it. If you could just move down towards her legs."

Sheeba shuffled down towards El's thighs and Shad came over and stood where Sheeba had been standing, on El's left side.

"I'm afraid you have to use quite a bit of force on two places in order to release this breastplate," said Shad.

He was talking once again for Ny's benefit.

"I have to push with a lot of weight, here and here," said Shad.

He was pointing to the middle of her chest just below her neck and to her left side down by the lower ribs. Shad placed the palms of his hands at both of those positions. Then he lifted them up and turned around to look at Ny.

"It's going to look aggressive, but you really do need to give it a lot of force for it to release the clamps. It won't hurt her and it is the official procedure for removing this portion of breastplate without damaging any underlying parts."

"I understand," said Ny, "and I trust you."

Shad nodded and turned back around. He placed his left hand just below her neck and slightly right of her sternum and his right hand just on the side of her lower ribs on her left side. He had to move her arm off the bed she was on so that it hung loosely pointing towards the floor of the van.

"OK, here goes," said Shad.

He leaned in, extended himself upright again and with a quick, forceful motion pushed down on his left palm and in on his right with great effort. So much effort in fact that the van swayed. It worked and the breastplate, like the skull plate before it detached and lifted off El's underlying frame by a couple of millimeters.

"You weren't kidding," said Ny to the back of Shad's head.

Shad nodded his head.

"No, you really do need to put some effort into it," said Shad, not looking at Ny but grabbing El's breastplate by the corners where his hands were and lifting it up and off the underlying Animae frame.

The underlying frame or body of El was the same shiny, slick, solid silver that matched her skull. There were similar indentations that looked haphazardly placed on the portion that you could see. There was, where the human heart might be on a real person, the female end of the pattern that would accept its male equivalent from the EEK. However, it all looked like a solid piece of metal. There were no borders that defined where the HEART was.

Shad pointed this out.

"It all looks like one piece," he said, speaking primarily for Sheeba's benefit. "But once the EEK meets that HEART you'll see it pop right up and you'll be able to remove it quite easily. But just wait until I give you the signal. The alarms will start going off, silently, but aggressively as soon as you place the EEK on the HEART, so let me get ready first."

Sheeba nodded and watched Shad go and sit back down. He picked up his P-Mac and tapped away at if for a few moments. Then he looked up at her.

"OK, I'm ready whenever you are," he said.

Sheeba nodded. She reached into the cabinet and pulled out the EEK. She looked at the male end, it was very intricate. Not much larger than a dice and the pattern was complex. It reminded her of pictures of mandalas she'd seen that Buddhist monks had created a long time ago. Only this pattern was of an abstract nature. She pulled off the clear cap that protected the pattern. She put that back into the cabinet. She looked over at Shad again and he nodded. She started to bring the EEK towards the HEART. Her heart was beating a little faster than normal. This was really it. They were about to create SAM.

"Shit," said Clarity, "stop everything you're doing."

Sheeba stood up and pulled the EEK away from the HEART. It hadn't yet made contact.

"I can't fucking believe this, we're getting pulled over again," said Clarity.

"Do you think they're onto us?" asked Ny. "But how would they know?"

"Let's just all remain calm," said Shad. "I don't see how they could be onto us. I think it's just a bit of bad luck, but once we get through this I'm sure it'll be smooth going."

He stood up and turned towards his wife and put his hand on her shoulder.

"Remember, you're just out for another test drive. By yourself because you want to make sure everything is going well before you and I go on a road trip down to Los Angeles later. They're not entitled to get into the back but you can pretend to try and let them only it'll be locked."

"I know, darling," said Clarity. "I'll try and make it as quick as possible."

Shad leaned in and kissed her on the side of her head.

"Rak, you might want to hop into Sheeba's chair. You'll be more comfortable," said Shad.

Rak did that, and as soon as he was seated in Sheeba's chair, Shad tapped away at his P-Mac and the screen between them and Clarity came down. They were now trapped in the back of the van and everything had locked them in.

"We don't have to be especially quiet," said Shad. "I installed some pretty robust sound dampening so we can't be heard from the outside."

Everybody nodded but didn't say anything. Ny's calm had evaporated like rock shocker's sweat on Hellas Planitia in the midday Martian sun.

# In the Shadow

When SA Lokilld arrived at Shadoelayke's apartment complex, MAAM Dredd and MAAM Kraken were waiting at the pod port by the elevators. SA Lokilld was happy for that. At least these skinjobs listened when you told them to do something. Not like some people he knew.

SA Lokilld and A Mortellen got out of their pod and walked over to where the MAAMs were.

"Have you located them at all?" asked SA Lokilld.

"No, Senior Advisor, we've waited down here as per your instructions."

SA Lokilld nodded.

"Then we'll all go up together."

He tapped his P-Mac and called the elevator for Shad's penthouse suite. It was waiting for them on the pod platform level. SA Lokilld knew that because the doors opened up a second after he'd called for the elevator. As they stepped in, SA Lokilld thought about that. Could it be coincidence that the elevator was on the pod platform level? He doubted that. Unless this penthouse elevator was malfunctioning it should be waiting on the last level that it dropped Mr. Rayzir and Ms. Downstorme off.

SA Lokilld turned to A Mortellen as they drove in the elevator up to Shadoelayke's penthouse.

"I think we're on an oiled skinjob chase," he said.

"I don't understand, SA Lokilld," said A Mortellen.

"Why was the elevator on the pod level? You saw how quickly it opened up the doors as soon as I called it. That means the elevator was at the last level that it dropped Mr. Rayzir and Ms. Downstorme off. If that's the case, then they won't be home."

"I see your point, Senior Advisor," said A Mortellen, nodding at the elevator doors.

The MAAMs stood silently behind them. Always watching, always listening, thought SA Lokilld. He was constantly aware of those ever-listening slippery, silicon snakes and tried to limit his conversations when around them. He hated it. He hated them. But that wasn't important now. What was important was to get off the Mars damn elevator and find out where Shadoelayke and Clarity actually were.

It seemed like the elevator was trying to climb up a cliff face as on old man with only one arm. At least that's how it seemed to SA Lokilld. But the actual reality was that it only took twenty-two seconds to climb those fifty floors to the penthouse. And then another five seconds as the elevator slid sideways, at least that's how it felt to SA Lokilld and A Mortellen.

"That's weird," said A Mortellen.

SA Lokilld shook his head wearily.

"No, I was hoping this would open up right into their apartment but I guess we don't have the authority," said SA Lokilld.

And when the elevator stopped and opened its doors they stepped out into a waiting room about the size of a large bedroom. There was a couch and a table in front of it with a handful of KTs on it. KTs were Knowledge Tableaus. Very similar to P-Macs but only a one way process. In other words, they were used primarily to access content from the GloNet without requiring any personal information.

SA Lokilld felt like he was in one of his own interrogation rooms, or what mentors colloquially called compliance cabooses or CCs for short. He could see no doors, or at least he couldn't identify the area that would open up and let them into the apartment.

On the left wall as he exited the elevator he noticed a portion of the wall light up and an image of an Animae dressed in a butler outfit greeted him. He was expecting a holographic projection, but they were more expensive.

"Welcome to chez Rayzir. How may I be of assistance, good sir?" inquired the obsequious butler.

SA Lokilld held up his P-Mac which showed his mentor credentials.

"These eyes are pixels they cannot see, I am blind to truth and to thee," said the butler.

"I am SA Lokilld with Mentorship K Division, Bureau of Interficial Crime. Permit SAGL-40-1701."

"Well, well, well, aren't you a very good boy and I see how keen you are. You must be pushing for a promotion. I was only kidding when I said I cannot see. I am not blind, I know full well of your notoriety."

The butler's upper crust English accent was gratingly getting on SA Lokilld's nerves.

"Now listen here, you pompous penile pervert. I want to see Shadoelayke Rayzir or Clarity Downstorme."

SA Lokilld was poking the image of the butler in the eye.

"My dear sir, if you prick us, do we not bleed? If you tickle us, do we not laugh? If you poison us, do we not die? And if you wrong us, shall we not revenge? You will be responsible for any damage caused to my unimatrix zero one."

"For the slippery stones of Sisyphus," said SA Lokilld. "Tell Mr. Rayzir or Ms. Downstorme that mentorship is here to see them."

"But they do not wish to see you. So I beg leave of you, good sir, if you will be on your merry way."

SA Lokilld hit the butler right on the nose with the side of his fist.

"I'm going to see if they're even in," said SA Lokilld to A Mortellen without looking at him.

He pulled out his P-Mac and started tapping at it, readying it for a scan of the apartment.

"Tut, tut, tut, Garrot. May I call you Garrot? How about Gary? No, Gar? No, you don't like that either. G-dog, no, no, wait, I've got it. G-string, yes, that's quite fitting, pun intended. Now listen here, G-string, unless you have a warrant you can't scan my employer's home."

"For all the sniveling sluts of Saturn why won't this Mars damn piece of silicon slag work," yelled SA Lokilld.

"It's like he said, Senior Advisor, we need permission. Let me request permission," said A Mortellen.

SA Lokilld nodded and looked at the staring butler.

"Are they in?" asked SA Lokilld.

"In or out, surely they are all about. But I cannot tell, my lips are sealed with a magic spell."

SA Lokilld unholstered his buzzkill and started beating the wall that the butler's image was on, furiously.

"That's a thousand New Dollars, G-string, and one thousand more," said the butler. "Do I hear three thousand? Yes, that man over there, G-string with his billy club held high in the air. Five thousand, oh I say, how rare..."

The butler went on like that as SA Lokilld beat at the butler's image with ferocity and all the pent up disappointments that SA Lokilld had experienced in his life. By the time he had tired the butler had informed him that the damage came to twenty-one thousand and three hundred New Dollars. That included the GUT CUT. The GUT CUT were the two taxes that were on everything. They stood for the Government Underlying Tax and the Consumption Underlying Tax. And it's really on everything. Everything except the GBA, the basic allowance. But any earnings or expenses are subject to both the GUT and the CUT. The GUT was twenty-two percent and the CUT was twenty-percent.

This is what the GoE required to keep the civil society that they thought everyone enjoyed. Services cost a lot of money, especially the Bureau of Mentorship. They took up a good chunk of the government's coffers.

SA Lokilld stepped back, breathing hard. He didn't see any damage to the wall at all. That didn't matter. He assumed that the butler was assessing costs based on the well established HIT law. Hooligans Instigating Trouble law. It was developed back in the early days when the GMIs were being developed. Shortly after the turn of the century the HIT law came into effect.

It came into effect because the citizenry were turning against the idea of genetically modified individuals. They had taken to breaking things and rioting whenever they could. The HIT law, many would argue, was so successful because you didn't have to destroy anything, you only had to have the intention to destroy something. And mathematicians had developed complex formulas for determining the cost of damage to things that remained undamaged. And this is why SA Lokilld had now been assessed fifteen thousand New Dollars of damage when none had occurred. And then add the forty-two percent tax and he had a big bill to pay.

But SA Lokilld wasn't all that worried. At worst, he'd be put on administrative duties for a month or six weeks and mentorship would pay the HIT charges. That was the worst case. The best case, which he believed would happen would be finding Nytewynd Blak, the skinner, and his cronies, and if that included Shadoelayke Rayzir then all the better. Catching a big fish like that would certainly get SA Lokilld a promotion and would be an embarrassing black eye against VM. And that meant that Mr. Rayzir's arrest would likely be overturned and quietly packed away. All the more reason to promote SA Lokilld to keep him quiet.

"Um, Senior Adviser, they won't give us permission to scan the interior of Mr. Rayzir's home without more evidence that we believe he's not inside," said A Mortellen.

"For the sickly sweet stink of sycophantic submissive servants," spat SA Lokilld. A Mortellen tried his best to stall a chuckle. SA Lokilld turned to look at him.

"Did you tell them that we've just come back from both Nytewynd Blak's apartment and Raklin Orbiter's place and all four of them were not there and yet their P-Macs were? Did you tell them that?"

"Yes, Senior Adviser."

"Did you also tell them that the calendars of Raklin Orbiter and Sheeba Brayvlin showed them attending with Nytewynd Blak and his skinjob to Sha-doelayke's apartment."

"Yes, Senior Adviser, but they say unless we have evidence to suggest that none of them are here, then we can't scan to verify."

"For the love of the suckling she-wolf's babes, Romulus and Remus, can we get any Mars damn help from them at all?"

"It doesn't appear so, Senior Adviser."

"Can we just ping the ever loving logs of Shad's P-Mac?" asked SA Lokilld.

"No, Senior Adviser, they won't let us."

"For the cherries from vestal virgins, I'll do it my Mars damn self," said SA Lokilld.

"Senior Adviser, I'm not sure that's a good idea," said A Mortellen.

SA Lokilld looked over at his colleague with eyes as hot as Venus.

"Do you not want to catch this skinner, Mortellen?"

"No, I do."

"Then sometimes you have to find ways around the roadblocks."

A Mortellen said nothing else. SA Lokilld tapped away at his P-Mac and then turned back to A Mortellen.

"I know a guy who works at MENSA, he can ping it subtly and let us know. We're just talking about a Mars damn ping, Mortellen. I just want to know where he is. If he's here, then that's on me. If he's not, then we've got them."

"Do you understand, my dear sir, that I am recording our whole interaction and you've just disclosed to me that you're about to commit an illegal act," said the butler.

"It's not illegal to ping someone's P-Mac to find out where they are, you obsequiously oiled oversized image of a buttock's boil," said SA Lokilld.

And SA Lokilld was not wrong. It wasn't strictly illegal, though he had been told not to. Well, actually, A Mortellen had been told not to. SA Lokilld hadn't heard a thing. At least not first hand. That meant at worst, this evidence might be thrown out of court. But he doubted that would happen once SA Lokilld had delivered a skinner to them. The courts were aggressively punishing skinners and the more that mentorship brought forth to the courts the happier they seemed.

SA Lokilld stared at his P-Mac after he'd requested the ping. As if the act of staring would make things go faster. But the truth was, he didn't feel like arguing with A Mortellen anymore. A Mortellen wasn't going to argue with him either.

The only reason that A Mortellen had told SA Lokilld that pinging wasn't a good idea was just in case there was fallout from it. At least he'd have been shown to be a voice of reason. He liked his Senior Adviser, but he wasn't going to be the fall guy for SA Lokilld's somewhat gray procedures. But A Mortellen was just as eager to rid the world of skinners as SA Lokilld. And that's what he was focusing on.

Pots really didn't seem to boil any faster when watched, thought SA Lokilld. His life was an interminable wait at the never ending well of bureaucracy. And then it happened, he got a notification from his guy at MENSA.

"OK, A Mortellen, are you with me or am I going to get the glory all for myself?"

"I'm with you, SA Lokilld."

"Good. I just got the location of Shad's P-Mac. Last seen at 42.958671 by -115.457860. That's just outside Hammett. Let's go."

SA Lokilld turned to step back towards the elevators. Before he did so, he gave the butler the middle finger. That was met by double middle fingers from the butler.

"May you forever swivel on the raspy thorns of Caesar's crown," said the butler.

They stepped into the elevator, the MAAMs and all, and SA Lokilld turned towards his colleague.

"Remind me that before this is all finished, I want to delete that butler from the face of this earth," said SA Lokilld.

"Yes, Senior Adviser," said A Mortellen.

They rode the rest of the way down in silence until they stepped off the elevator onto the pod platform. SA Lokilld looked down at his P-Mac again. It was T0157.

"What is he doing out there near Hammett at almost two in the morning?" asked SA Lokilld to no one in particular.

"Probably driving around in that combustion vehicle his wife built," said A Mortellen.

SA Lokilld started nodding slowly and then faster.

"Yes, A Mortellen, I believe you're right. And if they've got Nytewynd Blak and Raklin Orbiter with them they can't be up to any good. And that Mars forsaken skinjob is probably with them. I bet they're having a moving meeting of the Animate executive. Which means that Mr. Blak is either part of that group or being inducted into it. This catch of ours, A Mortellen, is looking better all the time."

"Yes, Senior Adviser," said A Mortellen, and he was thinking along the same lines. If they could catch a skinner and a handful of the big fish involved with Animate, their futures were very bright.

"Let us head that way and I want a MOLE sent out too," said SA Lokilld.

"I'm already on it, Senior Adviser," said A Mortellen. Tapping away on his P-Mac and requesting a MOLE from dispatch. MOLE being another acronym for Mentors Ongoing Lookout Emergency broadcast.

# Black Night Blues

N y felt the van drift over to the side of the road and eventually stop.
"There's nothing wrong with El being exposed like that is there?" asked Ny.

Shad shook his head.

"No, Eve's fine. She could stay like for a long time. Eventually you'd need to apply more silicon lubricant and clean her up but that's if she's like this for weeks. We have nothing to worry about other than these goddamn jackboots," said Shad.

"We're so close," said Ny, "I'd hate to see it end before it's begun."

"Me too. At least at this stage. I want to see the journey completed," said Rak.

"We'll complete it, my love," said Sheeba. "My fingers are itchy and this harness makes me feel very confident. As soon as this turgid jackboot leaves it won't take us long at all."

Clarity waited in the front seat all by herself. She could see the pod stopped behind her by about five or so meters. The blue and purple lights blinking on top of the mentor pod from right to left indicating the side that traffic should stay to.

Nothing happened for a long time. She couldn't see into the pod on account that there weren't really any windows on it.

"Good evening, no, good morning, mentor. How may I help you?" said Clarity, practicing her sincere and most genuine surprise at being pulled over. She was nervous. Who wouldn't be?

Why was she being pulled over again? Twice in almost as many nights. Maybe these jackboots were just bored and wanted a closer look at Mr. T. Maybe she was just unlucky. I mean nobody knew what they were up to. They'd only been gone under an hour and as far as anybody was concerned, she was still at home with her husband. At least that's where her P-Mac was.

And that got her even more nervous. Ideally she had her P-Mac with her. She didn't strictly need it if she was traveling in this combustion vehicle from where she had last left her P-Mac. But her P-Mac was at home, not at the hangar. Surely the mentor would figure out that she should have come from the hangar and not from her apartment complex in Boise. So why was her P-Mac not at the hangar?

She was overthinking it. Maybe, if she was lucky, she was getting a lazy mentor who only wanted to take a look at her van. She could dream, couldn't she? Before these last couple of nights she had a hard time remembering the last time she had to interact with a jackboot. Sure, she'd been involved in MEFF for many years and from there she'd gotten involved in MIM which was where she met her husband. But she'd always played supporting roles. She'd never been in the thick of it, in the trenches so to speak.

She didn't like the jackboots because she'd seen firsthand how they treated certain groups of people. Skinners especially. She never understood the obsessive hatred and never-ending pursuit of those who loved machines. What were skinners doing that was so awful or harmful? Nothing really. The GoE was just scared of it. Maybe because they knew if you allowed interficial relations eventually someone would want to give the Animae complete sentience. Well, maybe they were right to fear that, thought Clarity as she waited.

Here she was, with her husband and Ny, the man who would be the first to free the Animae if they didn't get shut down by these jackboots. But really, what was the harm of allowing more inclusion, more love in the world. She understood that things could go wrong if you freed the Animae. Maybe they would end up annihilating humanity. But you couldn't say we didn't have it coming to us. But maybe if love was allowed to flourish between humans and Animae, maybe nobody would feel like the Animae were being treated like second class citizens. And just maybe, if everyone could love how they wanted there'd be no need or desire for full Animae sentience. Problem was, that outcome could never be explored. It was nothing but pure speculation on her part.

In her side mirror she saw the mentor step out from the left side of the pod. In the passenger side mirror, another mentor stepped out and walked towards her passenger side. She kept her hands on the steering wheel. The mentor walked up towards her door. Clarity rolled down the window.

"Good morning, mentor," she said, looking at his breast pocket where his name was embroidered. It read, A VERVALIK.

"Good morning," he said. It was hard to tell what he looked like behind the air scrubber. It masked his features just as it did hers. But his voice, if Clarity was reading it right was on the friendlier side of fascism.

"This is a nice ride," he said. "I want to say it's an early to mid nineteen eighties GMC van."

"Thank you, Adviser. You're right. It's a nineteen eighty-three GMC Vandura van. The G15 version. It was made popular by the nineteen eighty-two television show called The A-Team."

A Vervalik shook his head.

"Never heard of it. I prefer current day holostreams. Short format or long format. Just give me a good show."

"I love those too," said Clarity, trying curry favor. "Bullit Brayve and Justice For All, is my favorite current short form holostream."

It wasn't a lie. Clarity did enjoy that mentor drama.

"Yeah, Bullit Brayve from the Bureau of Mentoring. Should be Mentorship. Don't know why they didn't get it right," said A Vervalik.

"I heard it was because it would have cost too much money to pay for the rights to use Bureau of Mentorship."

"Could be. Could be," said A Vervalik. "We don't just let anyone use the rights to Bureau of Mentorship. Can I see your license and authorization?"

A Vervalik remembered why he had pulled her over. It was actually to see the van. But he had to pretend that he was doing his job.

"I don't have my P-Mac with me. I left it at home," said Clarity.

"I'm assuming you have a port attached then?" asked A Vervalik, as he took his P-Mac from his belt and started to scan the van.

"I do, Adviser," said Clarity.

Clarity waited and watched as A Vervalik looked at his P-Mac which had brought up her license and authorization.

"Good," he said. "Your documents are in order."

He looked through the driver's window and across to the other side where his colleague was standing and he nodded.

"Who built this for you?" asked A Vervalik.

In her mind, Clarity did a huge eye roll. Even now, in the latter half of the twenty-second century it was still assumed that a woman wouldn't be interested in cars or their current equivalent.

"I did," said Clarity, "it says so on my authorization."

Her tongue was a little sharper than it might have been otherwise. Play nice, she said to herself, we need friends not enemies.

"Yes, I did see that. I wanted to find out if it was true. I'm a bit of a grease monkey myself."

"Really," she said, feigning interest. It wasn't that she didn't enjoy talking about cars. In fact she loved it. She was on gearheadz.movement.global almost daily. There were lots of ecclesia or groups on GloNet devoted to all sorts of things including vehicles. Gearheadz was the most popular for combustion vehicles. Electrified.movement.global was the most popular ecclesia for electrified vehicles.

"Yes, in fact I'm putting the finishing touches on my twenty ninety-nine Wattz Shark. Are you familiar with it?"

Clarity was familiar with it. It was one of the most popular electric vehicles of the late twenty-first century. The design in those few decades around the late twenty-first and twenty-second centuries had reverted back to the era of the nineteen fifties, it seemed. Or at least the futuristic prototypes of what future vehicles might look like. Take the Y2099 Wattz Shark. It reminded Clarity of the 1955 Lincoln Futura.

"The Batmobile," she said, smiling, not that A Vervalik could see her smile through her air scrubber but her voice carried its tone.

A Vervalik nodded.

"That's right actually. Though at the time I didn't know that. A friend had to point it out. I bought it for the styling."

Clarity nodded and continued to keep her friendly smile on her face. If not to be seen, at least to be heard in her voice's tone.

"So you're a bolt head," then said Clarity. Bolt heads being into electric vehicles.

"No, no, I'm a gear head, a grease monkey like you," said A Vervalik.

"Yes, you did say that, sorry. I thought you were just using it as a catchall phrase."

"No, I meant it literally. I'm on Gearheadz pretty much every day. A great community. Are you on?"

Clarity nodded. Her smile felt heavy and her patience felt like a headache trying to claw its way through her skull.

"What's your call sign?"

"P144YtheF001," said Clarity.

"No way, you're everywhere. You've actually helped me out a bunch of times. Do you remember when I asked you about the best tension setting for belts on my Wattz Shark?"

Clarity smiled and nodded a bit. She didn't remember that at all. She was one of the call signs with most letters on the site. She'd met a lot of people and helped most of them.

"You told me the exact number."

"I'm glad I was able to help," said Clarity.

"Mars, it's crazy to be talking to, pity the fool, in the flesh. I always thought you were a man. Don't get me wrong, women can do anything men can. Even still, in this day and age I've only ever heard about one other female grease monkey but I never met her in real life. So this is great. I've met a female grease monkey and you're pity the fool. Mars damn this shift is starting out great."

A Vervalik wasn't helping himself, thought Clarity, so she figured she'd help him out of his bind.

"What's your handle again?" she asked.

"Right, I didn't tell you. It's HillStreetBlues33," said A Vervalik. "The thirty-three on the end is the last couple of digits from my identification number. You probably remember that from when I showed you my credentials when I pulled you over."

Clarity put a gash on her face that was supposed to be a smile. It didn't feel as comfortable as a smile should be. Not that he could see it. She nodded at him too.

"Yeah, I've seen you around on the ecclesia," she said.

"Well, like I said. I'm on it pretty much everyday. Just finishing up the engine. Hoping to take it for a spin in a week or two. All going well."

"What kind of pistons did you put in it?" asked Clarity, trying to play along but hoping this was the end of the conversation.

"It's got a six liter, OHV engine with a three speed turbo drive automatic. It's going to fly."

"That sounds like the original engine they put in that model of Lincoln Futura," said Clarity.

"That's right. I wanted the authentic experience. Keeping the whitewalls too."

"Sounds like a lot of fun," said Clarity. "May the road rise up to meet you and the gas tank always be full."

"Ah, the gear head's blessing. Thanks. I appreciate that. Do you mind if I hop in and take a look from the driver's seat."

Before Clarity could answer, A Vervalik held his hand out to help her down and out of the van. Before she knew it she was standing on the road in front of the open driver's door and looking at A Vervalik in her seat holding onto the steering wheel.

# Grand Theft CEV

"Did you give it a nickname?" asked A Vervalik, yanking on the steering wheel.

"Mr. T," said Clarity.

A Vervalik upturned his mouth and nodded.

"What's it mean?"

"Doesn't mean anything, it's the name of the character in The A-Team. That show where the van's from."

A Vervalik nodded, eyeing out the dash in front of him.

"Mr. T, you said. That's the name of a person? Really?"

"Well, yeah, sort of. Mister is a salutation, like Adviser, but mister in those days didn't have to be earned. T is an initial of his last name. The actor's name was Laurence Tureaud."

A Vervalik was bobbing his head from side to side.

"Makes no sense to me. Those just don't sound like proper names and that salutation, bizarre. How could you not earn a salutation? You can't just give them away for free. They have to be earned."

"Things were different back then, Adviser. It was almost two hundred years ago."

A Vervalik nodded absentmindedly.

"What's your cars nickname?" she asked.

A Vervalik looked over at her.

"She's got a proper name, not like Mr. T. I call her SFS. Shark Fin Soup. But I usually just call her SFS, sfiss or even just essie."

Clarity smiled thinly and nodded. She didn't get it. Had he just insulted her about what she'd named her van or had she insulted Mr. T's moniker? Because that would be a pity for that fool.

And really, Shark Fin Soup as the name of a car? Now that was ridiculous. Sure you could name it whatever you wanted, but you usually gave it some sort of human name, and most often it was a female name. That's what the car nicknaming convention mandated. At least according to the CNC section five, paragraph three, sub-paragraph nine. And that last part was nonsense. There was no Car Naming Convention, at least as an organization. But you don't mess with history.

"Listen, I'm going to take it for a quick spin. You don't mind, do you?" asked A Vervalik as he started up the van, closed the door and drove off before Clarity could reply. Clarity watched him go. The red tail lights of Mr. T growing smaller and smaller as he sped away.

"That didn't take long," said Ny, holding onto the side of the bench he was sitting on as the van lurched forward.

"Not a graceful drive off, if you don't mind me saying so," said Sheeba moving less gracefully than before in her harness.

"Yeah, what do you think's wrong with Clarity?" asked Rak.

Shad brought his hand up towards his mouth. He concentrated on trying to listen. The van lurched forward, moved from side to side, and slowed down suddenly before speeding off again. Shad couldn't hear anything. If Clarity was speaking then he couldn't hear her, just as he'd planned the screen to be. Should he have the screen roll back up into the roof so he could talk to her? He wasn't sure. He was undecided. The longer the driving went on, the more Shad questioned whether it was really his wife driving.

"Don't you want to talk to her and let her know that we're still in the back?" said Ny, grinning. He was imagining Clarity speeding off from the crime scene, leaving the jackboots in her dust.

"I don't think it's my wife," said Shad, leaning in towards the center and whispering.

"I thought you said we didn't have to whisper?" asked Ny, whispering back.

"You're right," said Shad, switching to his normal voice. "I don't think Clarity's driving."

"Maybe we're getting impounded," said Ny, thinking back to all those old cop shows he'd watched.

Shad shook his head.

"I don't think so. I've never heard of the jackboots impounding a vehicle by driving it themselves. They call a tow pod to take the vehicle back to the pound."

"So what's happening?" asked Rak.

Shad shrugged.

"I don't know. But it's definitely not how Clarity drives," said Shad, as they continued to lurch back and forth in their seats, or harness, or hammock as the case may be. El was the most stable on account of her hammock being fairly fixed in place. "I just can't see Clarity driving like this, especially knowing that we're in the back."

"But we can't be sure. It would be nice to have a camera in the front compartment so we can see who's actually there," said Sheeba.

Shad nodded.

"There is a communication system to talk to us in the back. It's only a one way street though. Clarity knows how to access it from the main display. That's another reason why I don't think it's her. I think she would have contacted us by now."

"You should come and stand out of the road," said A Vervalik's partner, who was standing on the shoulder with her arms crossed in front of her.

Clarity nodded and walked over towards her.

"Does he always steal other gear heads' vehicles?" she asked, with a smile on her voice. She noticed the woman's name. She was also just an adviser. A SLYTHLINK was across her upper chest just above her left breast, embroidered on her uniform.

And that made Clarity wonder why jackboots didn't use more modern clothing. For example, construction workers, and not all of those jobs had been taken over by Animae, had to wear brightly colored, phosphorescent uniforms that had fibelite displays on them, front and back. Fibelite being intelligent fabric fibers that could be lit up separately in lengths as small as a fraction of a millimeter squared. It would display information to those around them about where to be in relation to the worker or what project was under construction. Time left before you could drive on or walk around. Those sorts of things. But for some reason, jackboots had opted for the old tech of embroidery.

The official reason was to provide security to the public so Mentorship said. They said that fibelite, at least when they looked into it, was too easily hackable which meant that jackboots, though they used the term "fellow mentors" could display a fake name and permit number if that information was displayed on a fibelite display on their uniform.

It made sense, but Clarity believed there were other reasons. It was cheaper, and maybe that helped keep costs down to spend on more MAAMs. Who knew, but at the moment it was on her mind.

Clarity offered her hand to A Slythlink. A Slythlink didn't take it so Clarity took it back and folded her arms in front of her chest like A Slythlink.

"I'm Clarity Downstorme," she said.

"I know," said A Slythlink, tapping her P-Mac on the side of her waist. "You'll get your van back. He's usually only gone about five minutes. We always have to pull other gear heads over so Rench can take a spin in their combustion vehicle."

"Rench, that's A Vervalik?" asked Clarity.

"Yes, Adviser Vervalik."

"I don't imagine you come across very many combustion vehicles, do you?"

A Slythlink nodded.

"Not too many. Maybe once a week. He's probably met all ninety-seven of you by now."

Clarity nodded.

"Are the combustion licenses still capped at one hundred and one?" asked Clarity. That was the number of total licenses and authorizations available for the Boise area. For a population of over ten million, that wasn't very many.

A Slythlink nodded. She didn't add any more to the conversation and Clarity was getting tired of pumping dry wells. She was also getting a little nervous and worried about the time. She knew that mentors were contacted every five minutes when engaged with the public and she was pretty sure they probably had been stopped for around five minutes.

And just as she thought that, she noticed A Slythlink tap her right ear. She heard A Slythlink speak her permit number and indicate that they were still on this CVS. CVS being shorthand for combustion vehicle stop. At least that's what Clarity imagined it to be short for.

The longer that A Vervalik was away with her van the more nervous she got. At least he wasn't driving with consideration of the passengers he had in the back. At least that would tell Shad that it wasn't her driving and hopefully he wouldn't do anything stupid. But the time rolled on. It felt like the time was longer than five minutes, and when A Slythlink tapped at her ear again to re-confirm they were still on the CVS, Clarity started to get even more nervous.

This time she heard A Slythlink tell whoever was on the other end that A Vervalik was "inspecting" the other vehicle. That made Clarity think that A Vervalik had probably taken Mr. T for a ride without proper authority.

Not that she cared particularly right at this moment. She'd just be happier to get the van back and be on their way. She wasn't about to rock the boat.

"What's going on?" asked Ny, knowing that everybody only knew as much as he did. "Seems like this erratic driving has been going on for five minutes or more.

"Almost five minutes," said Shad, looking at his P-Mac. "Just over four minutes now."

Shad's P-Mac vibrated in his hand. He looked down at it. There was a notification on his screen that he's just been pinged by a mentor P-Mac. He couldn't tell whose. This was something he'd set up a couple of days ago just as a security notification. It had been difficult to put together, because it meant that his P-Mac had to be listening to all traffic coming from and to his P-Mac and that meant encrypted traffic. And mentor-based encrypted traffic was difficult to decrypt. Some had said impossible. But when Shad heard impossible, he thought, rather, I'm possible. And that's exactly what happened. He'd found a bug in their algorithms he was able to exploit that unmasked their communication traffic.

"Shit," said Shad.

Ny looked at him with a furrowed brow.

"What?" he asked.

"I've just been pinged by mentorship. They know our whereabouts," he said.

"But they're right here with us," said Ny.

Shad nodded.

"Yeah, but I bet this is not them. I'm thinking this is probably your friend, that jackboot Lokilld."

"For the love of Trojan horses," said Ny. "That's Marsed up."

"That would be my guess. I can't tell who pinged. But who else is that focused on you?"

"You're right. Mars damn," said Ny. "Is there anyway you can stop them from pinging you?"

Shad turned off his P-Mac.

"I've just powered it down. That's the only way. But I'll have to power it up for us to work on Eve. Then they'll be able to ping us again and find our location. We're going to have to be quick once we start the transformation of Eve. We're going to have to be quick and accurate."

"What if he knows that we've also been stopped?" asked Ny. "Then we'll be detained until he gets here."

Shad nodded sadly with his mouth upturned.

"That's a concern for me too. The only saving grace is that a ping doesn't give that much information. He only knows our whereabouts at that moment in time. Nothing more. But if he's smart, and I think he is, he'll eventually request a pull from mentorship on any interactions with any of us from today, and that would give him this traffic stop info. We can only hope he doesn't think of that for a while."

Ny sunk into depressing thoughts. What they needed now to survive the next ten or fifteen minutes was a bit of luck and he wasn't feeling all that lucky.

Mr. T lurched violently to the side as A Vervalik pushed it to the limit as he tried to do a hard one-eighty in the middle of the road. Ny was pushed up against the sidewall he was sitting against. Shad and Rak had to grab onto their seats and Sheeba, in her harness, flew towards Ny, kicking him in the face with her feet. It caught him by surprise but it wasn't hard enough to draw blood on account that it wasn't done on purpose.

"Sorry," said Sheeba, suspended momentarily at almost a ninety degree angle.

As the van completed its turn, Ny was thrust towards the back of the van and Sheeba swayed towards that direction before coming crashing back down into the side of El's platform. She didn't hurt herself on account of the harness and gyro mitigating most of the effects of the momentum.

Ny was worried mostly about El. But she was strapped in which prevented her from falling off the firm hammock she was on. Her scalp and breast plates did come off her lower abdomen. Thankfully they landed on the floor of the van with their interiors facing up. Ny reached down and picked them up and put them on his lap.

"Maybe I'll just hold onto these," he said. "Is that jackboot being a Mars hole or does he just not know we're in here?"

"Probably a bit of both," said Rak, grinning.

After completing the turn and briefly coming to a stop, the van lurched forward and Ny could hear the growling engine get louder and faster.

"Clarity built this van to withstand this sort of abuse, right?" asked Ny.

Shad nodded.

"And hopefully that's where we're heading back to. Maybe this jackboot just wanted to take if for an inspection ride, except those have to usually be booked in advance unless he found something particularly worrisome which I'm pretty sure he didn't."

"Here they come," said Clarity, seeing Mr. T's white headlights far in the distance.

"They?" asked A Slythlink, staring at Clarity.

Clarity stared back. Shit, she thought, I shouldn't have said that.

"Yes, Mr. T and A Vervalik," she said, trying to put a smile on her face to mask any concern.

"You consider your combustion vehicle to be a person?" asked A Slythlink.

"Well, not exactly. You're not a gear head, right?" A Slythlink didn't say anything. "If you were," continued Clarity, "then you'd realize we do sometimes personify them. But it's just fun. I don't really believe the van is a person. But when you've worked on a combustion vehicle for two years like I have, you do start to feel connected to your work."

A Slythlink stared without blinking and without moving her head. Clarity looked away and watched as Mr. T's lights got bigger and bigger. When Mr. T was about twenty meters away, A Vervalik did another one-eighty bringing the van back to point in the direction it was when he'd pulled it over. Even in the light of the police pod, Clarity could see the smoke from her tires. She was not happy. But she wouldn't show it.

A Vervalik reversed Mr. T back to within a few meters of A Slythlink and Clarity. Then he turned off the ignition and jumped out of the van.

# Back on Track

**"** That is a lot more fun than it looks," he said. "That engine is quite powerful."

You could tell he was grinning by his eyes. They sparkled and they creased at the corners.

"Yeah, it's surprisingly more peppy than you'd think," agreed Clarity.

"You're not out there speeding now, are you?" asked A Vervalik.

"Of course not, Adviser. But I have taken Mr. T to the track before."

There was only one combustion vehicle track in Boise. It was called Skidz Road Ribbon.

A Vervalik slapped Clarity on the shoulder.

"I was just kidding with you. Very nice job you've done there on Mr. T. Weird name, but good combuv." Combuv was slang for combustion vehicle amongst gear heads. "I'd like to take a look in the back if you don't mind."

"Well, there's nothing in there. It's just an empty shell."

"Still, I'd like to take a look."

"Sure," said Clarity.

Clarity walked towards the side door of Mr. T when she saw A Slythlink tap her P-Mac and then tap her ear. That meant she was talking to someone in mentorship but her voice was muted from being broadcast outside of her air scrubber. In other words, Clarity couldn't hear what she was saying. A Vervalik looked at A Slythlink. That meant A Slythlink was probably talking to him. A Vervalik nodded and then looked back at Clarity. He walked over to the side of the van where she was.

"My colleague said you used the term 'they' when you saw me coming back towards us. As in, here they come. Why is that? Is there anyone in the back you're hiding?"

"I swear by Jupiter's lightning rod that it is just me and Mr. T out here on a test run tonight. I tried to explain this to A Slythlink, but I don't think she's a gear head, but I'm sure you'll understand. When I said, here they come, I was talking about you and Mr. T, my van. You know how it is that we sometimes personify our pride and joy. I've been working on Mr. T for just over two years now and I've sort of come to see the van as having a personality, if you will. You get that, don't you?"

Good save, she thought to herself. A Vervalik nodded.

"Of course, I understand," he said. "Still, I'd like to see in the back."

"Of course," said Clarity. She reached for the door handle and tried to slide it open. It wouldn't budge.

"Maybe it's locked," she said.

Clarity hopped into the driver's seat and pushed the power door lock button to unlock all doors.

"That should work now," she said, jumping back out and trying the door. It still wouldn't budge.

"Do you want to try?" asked Clarity.

A Vervalik tried opening the sliding rear door. It wouldn't budge. He yanked on it as hard as he could.

"Seems like it's almost glued stuck. You haven't actually welded the door shut have you?"

"No, Adviser. Absolutely not. I plan on completing the back of the van in time. Maybe it's rusted stuck somehow. Let's try the back doors."

Clarity led A Vervalik to the back of the van. A Slythlink didn't seem to be involving herself too much. Clarity wasn't sure why. Maybe she didn't care for combustion vehicle stops.

Clarity tried the back door handle. It wouldn't open the doors. She stepped aside and A Vervalik tried the door handles. He also couldn't open them.

"I'm sorry about this, I just don't know what's happened. It's probably stuck from all the muck that's in the air."

"I thought you said this was the first time you'd taken it out?" asked A Vervalik.

Clarity shook her head.

"The first time I'd taken it out solo. I took it out a couple of nights ago with my husband and some friends. He didn't want me taking it out alone the first time just in case something happened. Funny enough, or maybe it's not so funny, but we were pulled over then."

A Vervalik nodded at A Slythlink and she tapped away at her P-Mac then she tapped at her ear and A Vervalik nodded again.

"I think it probably needs better lubrication on the door hinges. Thinking about it now, I really think maybe it's the atmosphere doing a number on the hinges. Also, sometimes I've been having problems with the electrical bits of this van. Let me get the keys and just double check that the back door lock is actually unlocked."

Clarity went around to the front and got into the driver's seat. She fiddled with the dash panel for a moment before finding the intercom setting.

"If you can hear me Shad, I think they're going to scan the back. I hope you can project an empty van interior to them."

Clarity took the keys out and dropped them on the mat by mistake. She leaned down to get them. When she opened the door again, A Vervalik was there. Clarity startled a moment.

"You gave me a fright," she said.

"Just seeing how you're coming along," he said.

"I dropped the keys in the footwell and I was having a hard time finding them without light. Here they are," she said, holding them up.

A Vervalik's air scrubber system had a couple of very small but quite bright lights on either side of his head. Clarity's didn't have that. Those kind were only available for mentors.

Clarity got out of the van and went round the back. She put the key in the keyhole and turned them left and then right. It locked, then she turned it back left again and it unlocked.

"I think the door was unlocked, but I've unlocked it again. Hopefully this works," she said, holding up her index and middle finger crossed together. She pulled on the door handle but the door wouldn't budge. She shook her head and tried again. She put a foot up against the rear bumper but it still wouldn't budge.

"I don't know what's wrong with this stupid door," she said.

"Maybe it needs your muscles," she said.

A Vervalik tried opening the door. He put both hands on the door handle and then put both feet onto the rear bumper and he pulled with all his might. The door wouldn't budge.

"Very frustrating," he said. "Would you let me scan the interior?"

Clarity smiled and shook her head slowly.

"I'm afraid not, Adviser. I think I've been very accommodating and I'm pretty sure you took my van without permission or authority. If you want to scan it, I need to see your authority for that."

A Vervalik wasn't happy. He tapped at his P-Mac and then tapped at his ear. He was probably telling A Slythlink to scan the van. That was Clarity's suspicion, but she didn't say anything. She did see A Slythlink work on her P-Mac and hold it horizontal which was the best way to scan and she did sweep it back and forth, trying to hide what she was doing.

"Then I'll get a warrant," said A Vervalik, turning to look at Clarity and stepping in front of her line of sight so she could no longer see what A Slythlink was doing.

A Vervalik tapped away at his P-Mac. When he was finished he looked back up at Clarity. Just over his right shoulder, Clarity could see A Slythlink finish up her scan and put it away. Clarity imagined that she'd sent the scan results to A Vervalik, but he gave no indication that he'd received them.

"This will only take a minute or two," he said.

Clarity wasn't concerned. They'd already scanned the interior, and they'd likely found nothing if Shad had done what he'd planned to do, which it appeared like he did. And even if A Vervalik got authority to scan the van, which she doubted, he wouldn't find anything either.

"We just got scanned," said Shad.

"Sisyphus' stones," said Ny. "That's not good."

Shad shrugged.

"They got nothing."

"Yeah, but now they want to start looking inside. Next they'll be impounding the van and we're all Marsed," said Ny.

Shad shook his head.

"I doubt it," he said. "This whole vehicle stop relies on very flimsy authority. We got pulled over, fine. But one of those assholes took us for a ride and that's probably illegal unless Clarity gave permission, and I know she wouldn't have given permission. Then, when you need to seek a warrant or other authority to look into a van on just a hunch you've got to have good reason and they don't. Additionally, if they try to bullshit their way with it, that won't work either because all logs will be sent, and their air scrubber systems are constantly recording as is their pod. They've just fucked themselves is what they've done," said Shad.

A Vervalik's P-Mac glowed a soft red. Clarity knew that meant that whatever he had requested had been denied. A Vervalik looked down at it and cursed under his breath. He had been denied and worse than that, he had been issued an official reprimand on his logs for having taken liberties with this CVS.

He looked up at her and put a smile back on his face to mask the tone of disappointment. Though he was happy that A Slythlink had done a reasonable scan. Not perfect, but what she'd managed to grab did show an empty shell of an interior. So Clarity Downstorme wasn't lying at least.

"Looks like I won't be getting that permission on this occasion. You're free to go. Make sure you get those locks fixed by your next inspection."

"Yes, Adviser," said Clarity, turning and walking back to the front of the van where she got in.

She started up the van and drove off slowly and carefully. In the side mirror she watched A Vervalik and A Slythlink conferring together with A Slythlink pointing to her P-Mac and A Vervalik looking from that to the back of her van and back again. Just as they started to be swallowed up by the polluted air, she saw them turn around and walk back to their pod. Clarity tapped at the main panel on her dash.

"We're free now," she said.

Shad tapped at his P-Mac and the screen between them and Clarity slid back up into the roof.

"Well done, darling," said Shad, turning and squeezing her shoulder.

"Did they scan us, Shad?" she asked.

"Yes, they did. But they didn't get anything."

"Good. That was a close one. Let's give ourselves a few minutes before we get back to the task. That was a bit nerve-wracking," said Clarity.

"Agreed," said Sheeba. "I could use a moment to recompose."

"Not too long," said Shad. "I got pinged earlier. About five minutes ago. I think it was jackboot Lokilld though I don't know for sure."

"Ah, shit," said Clarity. "I'm going to head onto the side streets. They won't be as smooth, but they'll probably be safer. Does that sound okay?"

"It's probably best. Sheeba can handle it, I'm sure."

"Are you keeping an eye out for another ping?" asked Clarity.

"No, sweetheart. I've powered off my P-Mac. The more pings they get from us the more they can determine our future trajectory. I don't want to give them that option."

"But they could also start putting out a request to MENSA or SEARCH and that would get them the CVS we just came from," said Clarity.

"You're right, darling, but I'm hoping in Lokilld's myopic hunt for Ny that he doesn't think of that right away, and by the time he does, that we're far away."

# Villainous Vitriol

The four of them were in the pod racing towards Shadoelayke Rayzir's location. SA Lokilld looked at the window in front of him. They were traveling at one hundred kilometers per hour. The time was T0201.

"How long until we reach our destination?" he asked.

The information appeared on the front window. They'd arrive at T0214. That wasn't good enough for SA Lokilld.

"I want to arrive by T0210," said SA Lokilld.

"You need authorization to travel faster than one hundred kilometers per hour in city limits, Senior Adviser. Once we're past city limits I will increase speed to one hundred and eighty kilometers per hour. That will get you to your location at T0212," said the pod voice.

"Unacceptable," said SA Lokilld.

He picked up his P-Mac and sent in a request for authorization to exceed predefined city speed limits. He had to give his reasons. And all of that took a minute. Another minute before he received authorization.

"Authorization to exceed city speed limits granted. Increasing speed to one hundred and twenty kilometers per hour. Maximum safe upper speed limit for the next five kilometers of mapped route," said the pod.

"Give me updated arrival time." said SA Lokilld.

T0210 appeared on the window in front of him.

"That's better," said SA Lokilld.

He looked down at his P-Mac again and tapped away at it. He was requesting another ping. If Shadoelayke Rayzir was on the road, that meant that he was likely traveling in a vehicle which meant he was on the move. SA Lokilld wanted to know which direction he was traveling. He watched and waited. It seemed like the universe grew a gray beard while he waited. Why he couldn't just ping himself was beyond him. The bureaucratic red tape drove him to madness at times. And this was one of those times.

Finally, his P-Mac vibrated. He looked at the screen. There was a notification on it informing him that the ping went unreturned. Current location of Shadoelayke Rayzir's P-Mac was unknown. It was T0204.

"For the soured milk from Juno's shriveled breasts, can I not get a taste of Fortuna's stingy favors?" said SA Lokilld, now bordering on pure rage.

"What is it?" asked A Mortellen.

"My last ping I just requested was unreturned."

A Mortellen nodded.

"Could be for a few reasons," he said.

"Enlighten me," said SA Lokilld sarcastically.

"There could be interference," said A Mortellen. "The area they're in could have a weak signal or Mr. Rayzir might have even powered off his P-Mac. Maybe it was running low on power."

What infuriated SA Lokilld about A Mortellen on occasion, was the younger man's willingness to give people the benefit of the doubt. He was a good mentor. But his ability to see the glass as half full all the time was maddening. All well and good when you were dealing with civil members of society. But when dealing with the likes of skinners and other depraved, criminals, such leeway was never a smart thing to do.

"I think the last option is probably the one we're dealing with," said SA Lokilld.

"Then there's nothing to worry about. I'm sure when we get closer to the location we'll pick up the signal again if he powers his P-Mac back on."

"But why would he power it back on just when we're in the vicinity?"

"Maybe he has air-gapped power in the van," said A Mortellen, hopefully.

"And if he has that, why isn't he using it now?"

"I don't know, Senior Adviser."

"I think he knows he's been pinged and that's why he's shut off the P-Mac."

"But that's impossible," said A Mortellen.

"Is it?"

"Yes, Senior Adviser. Our architects have found no bugs in the code that would allow someone to be informed of a ping."

"And that's what you believe?"

"Well, yes, Senior Adviser. They wouldn't lie to us."

"I'm not saying they're lying, A Mortellen, I'm saying that the VP of Practical Intuition and Logic at VM is a man who is likely one of the best architects here on Continent NA, if not on the entire globe. There is a distinct possibility that he has figured out a way to do it. And if these Mars holes are part of Animate, which is what I think, they'd want to be especially careful."

"I see your logic, SA Lokilld. So what can we do?"

"I will wait a couple of minutes more and then I will ping again. If I get no response I'm requesting all available pods to descend on the area."

"That sounds like a great plan, SA Lokilld," said A Mortellen, trying to get back into SA Lokilld's good graces. He disagreed with his colleague. He didn't think SA Lokilld was thinking clearly. He didn't think this was as big a conspiracy as SA Lokilld thought it was. In fact, A Mortellen didn't even think they were on the heels of leaders of Animate. At best, they were after a couple of skinners. Still a worthwhile collar for both of their jackets, but not an Earth-tilting win.

In fact, why would the leaders of Animate have a moving meeting in an old-fashioned combustion vehicle? It didn't make any sense. They'd probably have it in a holorized environment masked as a coffee shop or even a bar. Not on a moving vehicle out in the middle of nowhere with the risk of getting pulled over by a pod or two. And that gave A Mortellen an idea.

"I've just thought of something, Senior Adviser," said A Mortellen.

SA Lokilld was tapping away at his P-Mac again.

"Just a minute, A Mortellen," he said, not taking his eyes away from his P-Mac.

It was T0208 and SA Lokilld was trying another ping. He waited. At T0209 the notification came back informing him that the ping had been sent and not come back.

"I swear upon the strength of Hercules' baby finger I am going to lose my mental matter," said SA Lokilld to no one in particular.

"I have an idea," said A Mortellen.

If I wanted your ideas, I'd give them to you, thought SA Lokilld. They were less than a minute to where the first and only ping had been located.

"Yes, A Mortellen, what is it?"

"If they're out here somewhere in a combuv, maybe a traffic pod has spotted them or perhaps even better, they were pulled over?"

SA Lokilld thought about it for a minute. Sometimes, out of the mouths of babes came pearls of wisdom. He had been so caught up and fixated on finding this skinner and perhaps soon to be leader of Animate that he hadn't thought of that.

"We have reached the destination," said the pod, as it slowed down and pulled over to stop at exactly the spot where Shad's P-Mac had received the first ping.

"Good idea," said SA Lokilld. "I'll put out a request."

He tapped on his P-Mac. Now he had to wait to hear back from dispatch.

"Keep scanning the roadway," he said to the pod.

"Burnt rubber has been identified on the roadway four meters up ahead," said the pod.

"Drive there and investigate further," said SA Lokilld.

The pod drove up slowly and back onto the road. It drove over the area where A Vervalik had done his hard one-eighty in the middle of the road. It scanned the rubber residue left there.

"Keep following the trail of rubber," said SA Lokilld.

The pod continued on back towards where they'd come from and then it turned around where A Vervalik had done his second one-eighty. It was now facing the same direction as it had been when it originally came to a stop. The pod drove up a little further then stopped.

"Rubber trail ends."

At the same time, SA Lokilld's P-Mac buzzed and pulsed a light blue. SA Lokilld looked down at it. A Mortellen looked over at his colleague.

"What does it say, Senior Adviser?" he asked.

SA Lokilld was reading the notification.

"They were pulled over here at T0152. They were released at T0207," said SA Lokilld. The time on his P-Mac was T0211. "That's just four minutes ago. Mars damn. If only Fortuna was my mistress instead of my madam. Tell me about the rubber."

"The rubber is fresh. Less than fifteen minutes old. The tires are four months old and are Mercury sixteen-inch Gripperz. The last direction of travel is east."

SA Lokilld nodded. He could have figured most of that out himself. He was happy with the last known direction of travel though. That was the direction they were currently pointing.

"Release the drones," said SA Lokilld, "and give them the type of combuv we're looking for, A Mortellen."

"Yes, SA Lokilld," said A Mortellen, beginning to get excited about the hunt ahead.

"I'm going to call for backup," said SA Lokilld.

SA Lokilld tapped away at his P-Mac. When there were other ears with him he preferred to type rather than speak his requests. Either way created logs of course, but he preferred keeping the MAAMs out of earshot whenever possible, and stuck in the pod with them, well, that wasn't possible.

While he waited to hear back about how many other mentors would join the glorious hunt, he heard the drones leaving the pod. There were two of them. He would have preferred three, but two was all each pod got so that's what he'd have to work with.

"Continue on the road we're on at one hundred kilometers per hour and head east," said SA Lokilld.

The pod started off and quickly got up to speed.

"Send the drones north and south of us. If they're not on this road, they're probably running parallel to it on one of the side roads," said SA Lokilld.

"Yes, SA Lokilld. But what if they started off in this direction and then headed onto the side roads and headed west?"

SA Lokilld looked at the time. It was T0212.

"Then send the drones west for ten kilometers. And then have them head back east to travel parallel to us. It's been five minutes since they were here. If they're traveling at eighty kilometers per hour which is the speed limit along here for combuvs they'd have only gone six or seven kilometers at the most."

"Yes, Senior Adviser," said A Mortellen.

SA Lokilld wanted to shake his head. A Mortellen was a loyal partner but for the love of Vesta's fire if he'd only use some initiative. But before SA Lokilld could get wound up about A Mortellen's lack of initiative he got a notification from dispatch. His request for backup was denied. HQ felt that SA Lokilld's evidence that Ny, Shad, Sheeba and Rak were leaders of Animate was clearly lacking anything substantial. And if SA Lokilld was just after a skinner, well, they could pick Nytewynd Blak up at their leisure. There was no need for him to be collared right now.

SA Lokilld figured as much. This was exactly how the lack of support from HQ was going lately. True, he didn't have a ton of evidence that Nytewynd Blak was an Animate supporter let alone leader. And if you looked at Ny's logs and reports from VM, he was, by all accounts a diligent and hardworking architect. But still, if there was something that SA Lokilld had been blessed with, it was an intuition more reliable than a bloodhound's nose.

In fact, on his chest was one big tattoo of Minerva's owl. Call it a sort of wisdom if you will, but SA Lokilld's intuition had gotten him where he was in life. That along with hard work. And now he was being denied what was going to be a big prize. Not Mars damn likely.

"For the love of the oracle's prophets whispered into Apollo's ears why am I being prevented in my pursuit of these Mars damn skinners and Animate leaders?" asked SA Lokilld to nobody in particular.

"They just don't believe you," said A Mortellen, realizing too late that he probably shouldn't have said that.

SA Lokilld shot him a glare. Then he tapped his earpiece.

"Get me A Vervalik or A Slythlink," said SA Lokilld. "This is SA Lokilld, where are you? I see. I want you to join me in the hunt for that combuv. Why? Because it's full of Animate leaders and skinners. I don't care you're on a pod pullover, what's it for? A Mars damn low level light emission transgression. I swear by Vulcan's hammer that I will squash you with it if you don't get here now. Good. This will be a huge feather in your cap. You'll make Jupiter himself proud."

A Mortellen looked over at SA Lokilld.

"No sign of the combuv up to twelve kilometers west of us, SA Lokilld."

"I said ten you imbecile. You're wasting our time."

"They're well on their way back here. In fact they've already passed us," said A Mortellen pointing at the window in front of them which showed a map of where they were as well as where the drones were.

The drones would find the van first. They could travel at up to two hundred and twenty kilometers per hour at an altitude of two kilometers which gave them a great vantage point. Though drones were hardly that high in the polluted pool of atmosphere.

On either side of the window in the pod in front of SA Lokilld and A Mortellen were live feeds from the drones. They were flying at an altitude of a little over five hundred meters on account of the difficulty capturing imagery on the ground at a higher altitude thanks to all the particulate matter. In fact, the imagery they were capturing was filtered through advanced algorithms to clear up all particulate and false readings based on night vision and infrared cameras. But what it showed could have been a beautiful moonlit night from a century and a half ago.

Then the drones zoomed in on what turned out to be the very steady, constant speed of an eighty kilometer per hour combuv. SA Lokilld noticed it first.

"For the sweet kisses of baby Diana, we've found them, A Mortellen. This is going to be a glorious capture. How long until we catch up with the combuv?" asked SA Lokilld.

"Less than one minute. Approximately thirty-nine seconds," said the pod.

SA Lokilld grinned from ear to ear. He hadn't felt this happy since he'd set eyes on that skinner, Nytewynd Blak. What a day. What a day that would go down in his logs as the day that earned him his long awaited and hard fought for promotion.

"Send the live coordinates to A Vervalik," said SA Lokilld.

"Yes, Senior Adviser. This is well earned. This will get us promoted," said A Mortellen.

"Yes, it will, A Mortellen, yes it will. But let us not count our pixels before they're lit."

# Flee and Plea

**"** Looks like the road is fairly smooth so far," said Clarity. "Not sure it'll get any better than this."

On the screen in the middle of her dash the time was T0213. Ny was sitting on his bench, just behind Sheeba who was still in her harness. He had the pieces of El upon his lap. Her hair felt different, but maybe that was just him.

Having her chest plate and scalp on his lap didn't minimize the love he felt for her. If anything he felt closer to her. But that wasn't what was on his mind at the moment. No, he couldn't shake a feeling of great and deep sadness. Mourning. That was probably the more accurate feeling he felt. Yes, he was mourning their love for he felt all the more certain that within weeks, months, however long it took, El would be more advanced than him by orders of magnitude.

How could an ape love an ant or rather, how could an ant love an ape? How could a SAM love a human? He couldn't see it. He felt so vulnerable and limited in ability.

"How are you feeling, Sheeba?" asked Shad.

Sheeba turned and looked at him. She'd been staring down at the HEART, psyching herself up. She looked back down at El.

"I feel good. Mr. T is as smooth as glass. Let's create SAM," said Sheeba. "Life, although it may only be an accumulation of anguish, is dear to me, and I will defend it."

Shad looked at her.

"I don't understand," said Shad.

"Frankenstein," said Rak and Ny simultaneously.

"My favorite book, ever," said Sheeba. She turned and looked back at Shad. "I'm ready."

Shad nodded. He attached the tentacled extendable wires from his P-Mac to El's scalp.

"How's the current?" asked Shad, turning to look at Rak.

"Steady at 333.336," he said. "Hasn't move at all."

"Good, you shouldn't have any problems. That being said, keep watching and maintaining."

Shad looked back over at Sheeba.

"Whenever you're ready," he said, looking down at his P-Mac and getting ready to fight the alarms.

Sheeba picked up the EEK and held it steady in her hand. She held it vertically and started to lower it towards the HEART.

"When does the time start again?" she asked, concentrating on what she was doing.

"Only once you dislodge the E3C," said Shad.

Sheeba nodded and lowered the EEK onto the indented pattern on the HEART. It's just like a mandala, she thought to herself. Let us open up the universe and breath sentience into Eve.

The EEK felt almost magnetic as it mated with the HEART. And in a moment the EEK seemed to become one with the HEART. It felt fused. At that point she felt a subtle shifting of the HEART under her steady hand. It separated itself from what it was attached to and lines formed and small crevices that weren't there before. Sheeba pulled up on the EEK and with it came the whole HEART. It was a metallic box of some sort that was no longer than seven and a half centimeters to a side. As she lifted it from El's chest, it felt much lighter than it looked. The bottom of it was open.

"Great job, Sheeba," said Shad. "You can suspend that from one of those hooks on the ceiling.

Sheeba did exactly that. Ny looked at Shad, he had started tapping away madly on his P-Mac. Sheeba stared at the E3C. It looked exactly like her practice chips she had used a couple of nights before. Sheeba stared at it for a moment.

"No rush," said Shad, "but these alarms are coming fast and furiously."

"Sorry," said Sheeba. "I just can't believe this is really it."

Sheeba reached for her extractor tool which was hanging from it's gyro attached to the ceiling, next to the Anigloo tool and now also next to the dangling EEK and HEART.

Sheeba took the tool and steadied her hand. The gyro worked as it should and even the small bumps and swaying of Mr. T as it raced along the road were smoothed out so that Sheeba felt as if she were in her surgical theater steady and as alert as she'd be in surgery.

She lowered the extractor tool onto the E3C and a moment later it was released from the underlying bed it was attached to. Sheeba pulled it away slowly and turned it upside down to expose the underbelly of it that required fresh Anigloo.

"Shit," said Clarity. "We've got jackboots on our ass and drones in the sky."

"Give us as much time as you can," said Shad, sweat beading at the corners of his temples. "You can do it, Sheebs," he said, regretting his choice of a nickname for her.

Sheeba didn't hear. She was focused on the task at hand. She swallowed and steadied her hand that held the E3C. She reached for the laser knife and quickly sliced off the end of the Anigloo tube so that the Anigloo could flow. She reached up and grabbed the Anigloo tool with her hand and brought it down over the top of the inverted E3C. She steadied herself and breathed out a long sigh.

Ny was counting in his head. He was sweating and not only from the warmth he was feeling in the back of the van, but from his own nervousness. He knew from last time and he knew from before that even, that the mentors would ask you twice to pull over. If you didn't do that they'd send you a thirty second timer notification after which your combuv would be disabled and come to a stop on its own.

"I'm sorry, you're cutting out. Can you please repeat?" said Clarity, trying her best to try and buy them some more time.

"Pull over and stop. This is mentor pod MP-42. You have ten seconds to comply."

"It's a bad connection. I'm going to have to pull over so you can come and talk to me in person."

"That's what I'm ordering you to do," said a clearly exasperated voice.

Ny watched the back of Sheeba as her arms and elbows moved ever so slightly. She was adding the Anigloo now, he thought. And she was. Sheeba was oblivious to everything. She wasn't even consciously aware of the conversation that Clarity was having with the mentors. Ny had reached fifty-seven seconds when he heard Clarity curse.

"Shit, they've sent the countdown. We only have thirty seconds until we're disabled. I'm going to slowly start slowing down."

Nobody was listening to her except for Rak.

"Steady as she goes," he said. "Light as a feather. We're at a very vulnerable point in the resurrection."

"I understand," said Clarity.

And with that, Ny felt the van start slowing down but it was barely perceptible. He wasn't upset about it. If the jackboots disabled them at high speeds, the wheels locked and engine stopped and you came to a very quick and abrupt and violent stop that added a lot of screeching to the tires and flinging of bodies inside the vehicle. He'd seen streams of it on the dark net.

# Mercurial Malevolence

"Do you have the location, A Vervalik?" snapped SA Lokilld.

"Yes, Senior Adviser, we are on our way. We'll be there in fifteen seconds."

"Good, that will be shortly after us."

The time had just rolled over to T0214. Up ahead the distant red taillights of Mr. T could be seen.

"There they are," said A Mortellen, as giddy as a kid pointing at the ocean for the first time.

SA Lokilld didn't say anything.

"Do you think they know we're coming fast on their tail?" asked A Mortellen.

"If they don't, they're about to get a rude shock. Maybe literally," said SA Lokilld with dark humor in his voice. SA Lokilld tapped at the dash in front of him which was not much more than a screen. He pulled up communications.

"This is mentorship. Pull over."

He waited. Nothing happened.

"Sniveling skinning serpents," said SA Lokilld, "I think they're ignoring us."

"Maybe they didn't hear us the first time, SA Lokilld."

SA Lokilld shot him a glance.

"Not bloody likely," he said.

He tapped at the dash again.

"This is mentorship. Pull over and stop," said a louder SA Lokilld.

He waited five seconds. Nothing happened. He tapped the dash again and just before he spoke.

"I'm sorry, you're cutting out. Can you please repeat?" said Clarity.

"Who's that?" asked SA Lokilld.

The window in front of him lit up with Clarity Downstorme's demographic information including her photograph.

"Right," said SA Lokilld, "she would be driving."

He tapped at the dash again.

"Pull over and stop. This is mentor pod MP-42. You have ten seconds to comply."

Nothing at first.

"It's a bad connection. I'm going to have to pull over so you can come and talk to me in person."

"That's what I'm ordering you to do," said a clearly exasperated SA Lokilld.

SA Lokilld tapped at the dash and large numbers in pulsing red displayed on the side of the window that was in front of him. Clarity's information moved over to the left.

"They're slowing down, Senior Adviser," said A Mortellen.

"I should hope so, they have twenty-five seconds to comply. Ready Mercury's Caduceus, A Mortellen."

"Not Jupiter's lightning?" asked A Mortellen. "The Caduceus might be overkill, Senior Adviser."

SA Lokilld looked over at him.

"Am I stuttering, A Mortellen?"

"No, Senior Adviser."

"Then do as I ask. I want nothing left to chance. Jupiter's lightning can sometimes be ineffective and I'm tired of playing games with these skinners."

"Yes, Senior Adviser."

A Mortellen tapped away at his P-Mac and synced Mercury's Caduceus to the timer.

The Caduceus was not a weapon that was used often on vehicles. Hardly ever on pods, as Jupiter's lightning was sufficient to disable the pod's circuitry and bring it to an abrupt stop. But on combuvs sometimes Jupiter's lightning wasn't effective, in which case you brought out the Mercury Caduceus. But the protocol was to use Jupiter's lightning first. And there was a good reason for that.

Mercury's Caduceus was a blunt instrument. It sent a combination of EMP, shockwaves and concussive sound waves that were bounced off the road. In effect, all passengers in the combuv were knocked unconscious and the combuv itself was very often flipped on its side, or rarely, onto its back. The Caduceus was that powerful.

SA Lokilld watched the timer. Ten seconds left. The speed was now at fifty kilometers per hour. SA Lokilld in his pod was five meters behind them, and behind SA Lokilld was A Vervalik's pod.

SA Lokilld started to grin as he counted down. Three... two... one. Mr. T was at thirty kilometers per hour. The pod he was in swayed back and then forth slightly as Mercury's Caduceus sent the pulse. You couldn't see it, but you could see the damage it wrought. Especially as it blasted its way through the particulate matter in the air as if a small tornado just ripped through it.

The next thing that happened was Mr. T flipped over onto its side and slid across the road towards the shoulder for about ten meters until it came to a stop. It looked as if Mr. T had just ridden over a bomb that exploded under it's right rear tire. That's where Nytewynd Blak was sitting. SA Lokilld didn't know that on account that he hadn't scanned the van to see who was actually inside.

The mentor pods came to a stop, SA Lokilld's just half a pod length ahead of A Vervalik's. SA Lokilld tapped at his ear.

"Pod forty-two and pod nineteen," he said. He got almost instant confirmation. "Everybody behind me. I'm making first ingress. Understood?"

A Mortellen, A Vervalik and A Slythlink all agreed, and with that SA Lokilld stepped out of his pod as his air scrubber wrapped itself around his face. A Mortellen was at his right shoulder and A Vervalik and A Slythlink were just behind them followed by the MAAMs.

# Don't miss out!

Visit the website below and you can sign up to receive emails whenever Jason Blacker publishes a new book. There's no charge and no obligation.

https://books2read.com/r/B-A-RBB-JJMBB

BOOKS 2 READ

Connecting independent readers to independent writers.

# Also by Jason Blacker

**A Lady Marmalade Mystery**
Beggar's Pardon
Sins of the Father
Gandhi's Sorrow
Phantoms of the Pharaoh
The Baron at Bishops Avenue
The Priest at Puddle's End
Lady Marmalade Cozy Murder Mysteries: Box Set (Books 1 - 3)
Four Red Diamonds (A Lady Marmalade Mystery 4 Pack)
Heartless
Loose Lips
Misery's Company
Poisoned Heart

**An Anthony Carrick Mystery**
Fourth Wall
Fifth Estate
Sixth Sense
Seventh Son
Brotherly Love
Anthony Carrick Hardboiled Murder Mysteries: Box Set (Books 1 - 3)
First Feature
Money Ain't Nothing
All In

Four Ways to Midnight
Second Fiddle
Third Base
Washed Up

**Carbon Heart Silicon Soul**
Jupiter: Book 1
Juno: Book 2
Juventas: Book 3
Bellona: Book 4

**Head Case Trilogy**
Head Rush

**TaXI Adventure**
Ta.X.I. to Angola

**Standalone**
Can You Please Be Quiet
Dust on His Soul
Flowers For The Journey
Forever Famine
Livid Blue
My Son And I
Ruffled Feathers
Running Red River
When There Was One
Red Reign

The Enigma Evolution
Small Boy
Lady Marmalade Cozy Murder Mysteries: Box Set (Books 4 - 6)


Watch for more at JasonBlacker.com.

# About the Author

Jason Blacker was born in Cape Town but spent most of his first 18 years in Johannesburg. When not grinding his fingers down to stubs at the keyboard he enjoys drinking tea, calisthenics and running. Currently he lives in Canada. Under his own name he writes hard boiled as well as cozy mysteries, action adventure, thrillers, literary fiction and anything else that tickles his muse. Jason Blacker also writes poetry and daily haikus at his haiku blog. You can find his haikus and other poetry at his website **www.haiqueue.com**. For FREE books and to stay up to date and learn about new releases be sure to visit **www.jasonblacker.com** where you can find more information about his writing and upcoming projects. If you enjoy space opera in the tradition of Star Trek then take a look at Jason Blacker's pen name "Sylynt Storme". It is under the name Sylynt Storme where you can find both sci-fi and vampire fiction written by Jason Blacker. "Star Sails" is the space opera series and "The Misgivings of the Vampire Lucius Lafayette" is his vampire series.

Read more at JasonBlacker.com.

www.ingramcontent.com/pod-product-compliance
Lightning Source LLC
Chambersburg PA
CBHW050856180626
46814CB00007B/2772